Jesse looked Jillian up and down again.

"You keep surprising me."

"Is that bad?" she asked, meeting his gaze.

"No. I like surprises."

The look in his eyes sent heat sizzling across her skin. Jillian took a breath and relished the burn. What he could do to her with his eyes was like nothing she'd ever experienced before. "Me, too."

His eyes flashed. "Good to know."

Oh, boy. She turned for the door. He grabbed her upper arm, spun her around and pulled her in tightly to him.

"Surprise," he whispered just before he bent his head and took her mouth with the kind of hunger that vanquished anything that stood in its way.

At the first touch of his mouth, Jillian gasped, then sighed, lifting her arms to hook them around his neck. He parted her lips with his tongue and she welcomed it, tangling her tongue with his in a seductive dance that had her heart hammering in her chest and her blood rushing through her veins.

* * *

Rich Rancher's Redemption is part of the Texas Cattleman's Club: The Impostor series—
Will the scandal of the century lead to love for these rich ranchers?

Dear Reader,

It's always fun to be a part of a continuity. It's a chance for very solitary writers to spend some time with other authors, comparing notes and making sure we're all on the same page! But the Texas Cattleman's Club continuity series is special.

Being able to revisit the town of Royal and the many characters I've fallen in love with over the years is a treat. Royal and its citizens are so familiar to me, it's sometimes hard to believe they aren't real.

In *Rich Rancher's Redemption*, you'll meet Jesse Navarro, a rough and rugged kind of guy with a dark past. Jesse's committed to doing the right thing and taking care of his family above all else. And then he meets Jillian Norris and her tiny daughter Mackenzie. Jillian's had a hard life, but she's proud and confident, with a serious distrust of men.

Jesse changes all of that.

I really hope you love this book as much as I do. Please visit me on Facebook and drop by my website to say hello.

Until next time, happy reading!

Maureen

MAUREEN CHILD

RICH RANCHER'S REDEMPTION

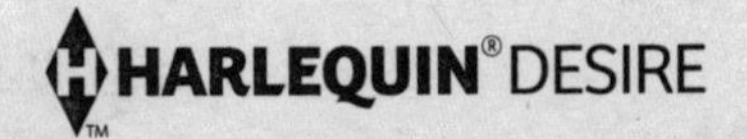

Special thanks and acknowledgment are given to Maureen Child for her contribution to the Texas Cattleman's Club: The Impostor miniseries.

ISBN-13: 978-1-335-97130-2

Rich Rancher's Redemption

This edition published by arrangement with Harlequin Books S.A.

For questions and comments about the quality of this book, please contact us at CustomerService@Harlequin.com.

Printed in U.S.A.

Maureen Child writes for the Harlequin Desire line and can't imagine a better job. A seven-time finalist for a prestigious Romance Writers of America RITA® Award, Maureen is an author of more than one hundred romance novels. Her books regularly appear on bestseller lists and have won several awards, including a Prism Award, a National Readers' Choice Award, a Colorado Romance Writers Award of Excellence and a Golden Quill Award. She is a native Californian but has recently moved to the mountains of Utah.

Books by Maureen Child

Harlequin Desire

The Fiancée Caper
After Hours with Her Ex
Triple the Fun
Double the Trouble
The Baby Inheritance
Maid Under the Mistletoe
The Tycoon's Secret Child
A Texas-Sized Secret
Little Secrets: His Unexpected Heir

Pregnant by the Boss

Having Her Boss's Baby
A Baby for the Boss
Snowbound with the Boss

Texas Cattleman's Club: The Impostor

Rich Rancher's Redemption

Visit her Author Profile page at Harlequin.com, or maureenchild.com, for more titles.

To all of my wonderful readers for
their support over the years.
It's because of you that I'm able to tell
the stories I love to write.

One

It had been two weeks since the funeral that...wasn't. Jesse Navarro still felt like the world had shifted beneath his feet. But, he assured himself silently, that was probably the normal thing that happened when your brother walked into his own damn funeral.

He frowned into the afternoon sun and told himself it wasn't easy to hold a fancy funeral when the guest of honor shows up. Alive. He pushed one hand through his hair and muttered, "Just be grateful, for God's sake."

And Jesse was. Grateful. Hell, he had his brother back. But he also had a damn mystery to solve. And Jesse didn't like mysteries.

If Will Sanders was alive and just now showing up in Royal, Texas, then whose ashes had been in the urn they'd believed was Will's? And who the hell was the guy who'd pretended to be Will for all those long months? And why did he do it?

"No," Jesse said aloud, "I know why he did it. The money." Hell, the Sanders name carried a lot of weight and not just in Texas. So the bastard had tried to cash in on Will's name and had done a damn fine job of it, too. It wasn't just Will's name he'd stolen. He'd had Will's face. Had his movements, his smile, down cold. He'd fooled Will's family.

Hell. He'd fooled *Jesse*.

That was a hard pill to swallow. Somehow, Jesse felt disloyal for not spotting the damn imposter the minute he'd shown up at the family ranch. How had he been duped? In his own defense, Jesse could admit that "Will" hadn't spent much time with the family. He'd avoided too much closeness and at the time, Jesse had just figured his brother had a lot on his mind.

Which, of course, he *had*. Or, the impostor had. The man had worked nonstop to keep up the illusion.

Jesse shifted his gaze to the main ranch house. A sprawling white mansion, it looked nothing like what you'd expect a ranch house to be. It was massive, elegant. All white but for the black shutters at the windows, the house boasted a wide, columned front porch and dormers on the second floor, and at night, the lights made it shine like heaven.

And somewhere inside that massive house, was the *real* Will Sanders. There were a couple of cars out front, and Jesse's gaze narrowed on one of them. It was a beat-up, faded green Honda with Nevada plates, and the woman who'd driven it was inside. With Will.

The woman, Jillian Norris, didn't fit her car. A woman like that belonged in a Porsche. Or at the very least a classic Mustang convertible. During all the chaos since Will's return, Jillian had somehow become a friend of Jesse and Will's sister Lucy, so she'd been at the ranch a few times. And every damn time, Jesse was slapped with an instant blast of heat that nearly swamped him. He'd spoken to her a few times, and her low, sultry voice had seemed to thrum in his blood, making it steam and sizzle in his veins.

He scowled at the distant horizon, telling himself that if he had any sense at all, he'd steer clear of Jillian Norris. Apparently though, common sense had nothing to do with what his body was demanding. Instantly, Jesse's mind drew up an image of Jillian and everything in him tightened. Shaking his head, he could admit to himself, at least, that it had been that way from the first minute he'd seen her at the funeral.

Drop dead gorgeous, with curves that could bring a strong man to his knees, Jillian Norris had mile-long legs and bright hazel eyes that looked both wounded and defiant. An interesting mix that had drawn Jesse in from the beginning. At the memorial service, she'd stood at the back with her baby girl. Yes, she had a daughter, about two. A miniature version of herself, with big hazel eyes, white-blond hair and a wide smile.

Jesse'd wondered, of course, who the hell the woman was and why she was at Will's memorial service. But then Will had strolled in, asked *What the hell is going on?* And suddenly there were much bigger questions that needed answering.

"And two weeks later, I've still got questions." Jesse shook his head, slapped one hand on the top bar of the corral fence, then squeezed the plank of wood hard enough it should have snapped in two.

His little brother was back from the dead and he was grateful for it. But there were gaps in Will's memories, leaving the family wondering exactly what had happened to him while he was missing. Naturally, Will wondered too, Jesse reminded himself, but somehow, it was harder to be on the sidelines. Hell, it was making Jesse crazy knowing there was nothing he could do to fix this situation. He was the older brother and he was used to riding to the rescue.

This time, though, no one had known a rescue was required and there had been nowhere to ride.

Chaos had erupted at the funeral, with Jesse's

mother shrieking Will's name and flinging herself, followed closely by Lucy, into the man's arms. Will had looked at Jesse for an explanation, but he'd been too glad to see his brother to find the words—and didn't know if the right words had existed anyway.

Shaking his head, Jesse remembered that it hadn't been until long after the confusion caused by Will's arrival had settled down some that he'd found out who Jillian was. Some lawyer had told her to come to Texas and claim a part of Will's estate on behalf of the child they'd made together. That little girl was a heartbreaker, but as it turned out, Mac wasn't Will's daughter after all. That had become clear the minute Jillian admitted that she'd never met the "real" Will before. Now she knew that like everyone in Royal, Texas, she'd met and been fooled by the impostor.

To give her her due, Jillian had been ready to leave once she found out the truth. But Will had convinced her to stay for a bit until this was all figured out. Jesse had quietly kept tabs on her and knew she and her daughter Mackenzie had been staying in a cheap motel outside Royal, and he imagined that being cooped up with a small child couldn't be easy.

Now she was here, meeting with Will, and Jesse told himself *he* should be in there, too. He gritted his teeth in frustration. But Will was as stubborn as he ever was and had insisted that this was *his* mess and he'd clean it up.

Still, that wasn't exactly true, was it? *Will* hadn't

done any of this. The impostor was the man to blame and if Jesse knew where he could find the guy—probably better he didn't know.

Still, he wasn't going to stand back and let Will try to untangle this wildly complicated situation on his own whether the man liked it or not. Jesse was and always would be Will's big brother. And damned if he'd let Will forget it.

He settled his black hat firmly on his head again and pushed away from the corral fence. He started for the main ranch house, his long-legged stride eating up the distance. His gaze swept across the palatial white home and as always, he felt that quick tug of gratitude.

He'd grown up here. From the moment his mother, Cora Lee, had married Will's father, Roy, the Ace In the Hole ranch had been home. Hell, Jesse could still remember his first glimpse of the ranch and the house that had, to a six-year-old boy, looked like a castle. All it had been missing were a few turrets, a drawbridge and a dragon or two, waiting to be slain.

And Roy had made sure Jesse and his younger sister knew, from that first day, that this was their house as much as it was Will's. That they were, all of them, *family*. And nothing was more important than that.

Family came first. One of the first life lessons drummed into Jesse, Will and Lucy as they grew up. And the one lesson that never changed or shifted. Jesse would do anything for the people he loved, which was why he wasn't going to leave Will swinging without support.

He'd already screwed things up pretty well with Lucy—but he wasn't going to think about that right now. Instead, as he climbed the steps to the wide, wraparound front porch, another life lesson popped into his head. His mother, Cora Lee Sanders, was hell on tidy, and living on a ranch had meant that she was constantly at war with dirt, dust and God-knew-what-else being traipsed into her house.

Wipe those feet before you drag a mess into this house.

In spite of everything, he smiled as his mother's stern warning echoed in his mind. But dutifully, Jesse scraped the bottoms of his boots on the wiry mat set out for that purpose, then opened the door and stepped inside. Instantly, the quiet wrapped itself around him and made him a little twitchy. Usually, this house was bustling.

Lucy and her young son, Brody, lived in the east wing, but four-year-old Brody had the run of the place and had never known a silent moment. Lucy was a single mom, and again Jesse had to struggle past twin pangs of guilt and regret at the thought. But his sister also had everyone on this ranch helping her out with the boy that kept all of them on their toes.

Jesse headed for the study, Roy's old office. Since his death, the whole family used it since Jesse hadn't been able to stake his own claim on the room in spite of being in charge of the ranch now. His boot heels hit the shining, hardwood floor in a series of taps that reminded him of a heartbeat, fast and hard.

The double doors were open, so he walked inside, subconsciously taking in the familiar room. Deep, maroon leather chairs, heavy tables and sturdy brass floor lamps. A thick rug with a map of the Ace In the Hole emblazoned across it, walls filled with books, and a bar where crystal decanters filled with whiskey, brandy and vodka glinted in the light. A river stone hearth simmered with a low-burning fire, and at the wide, broad desk sat Will, looking uneasy.

Opposite him, in one of the leather chairs, was Jillian Norris.

The instant Jesse's gaze landed on her, he felt a jolt of something hot and fierce slam into the center of his chest. The woman made a hell of a picture. She was tall, at least five foot ten without high heels. Her long, wavy blond hair was pale enough to look like spun gold, even caught up in the ponytail he'd rarely seen her without. Those huge hazel eyes of hers looked both wounded and defiant. An interesting mix that had drawn Jesse in from the beginning. The few times he'd seen her, Jesse had noticed the stubborn tilt to her chin and the light of devotion in her eyes when she looked at her daughter.

Will looked up at him. "Jesse?"

"Go ahead. Don't let me interrupt." He ignored the flash of irritation on his little brother's face as he moved farther into the room and took a seat in one of the chairs.

Will's frown only lasted an instant, probably because he knew it wouldn't have the slightest effect on Jesse. He focused on Jillian again. "If I could make this easier on you, I'd like to."

Jesse watched the woman. She looked…embarrassed, and he wondered if she'd had that expression *before* he'd intruded on this meeting. He should probably regret coming in here, but he didn't.

"And I appreciate it," Jillian said, her voice soft enough that Jesse had to strain to hear her. "But I've told you. You don't owe me anything. Mac's not your daughter." She took a breath, then sighed a little. "I know that now."

Will got up from behind the desk and walked around it. Leaning back against the front edge, he said, "I'm not her father, no. But the man who is was pretending to be me and that hits close enough to home for me that I can't ignore it."

She stiffened in her chair and folded her hands tightly in her lap. "Look, I don't need your help. Mac and I will get along fine—"

Jesse heard the pride in her voice and knew Will did, too, when his brother spoke next.

"This isn't charity, okay?" He flicked an impatient glance at Jesse, as if silently trying to tell him to go away.

Jesse shook his head.

Sighing, Will turned back to the woman who was saying, "What else would it be?"

"A favor," Will said. "To me."

She laughed, and even in this weird situation, Jesse's insides responded to that low, throaty chuckle. He shifted uncomfortably.

"You want a favor. From me." Disbelief rang loudly in her tone.

"Absolutely." Will laid his hands on his thighs and leaned toward her. "The bastard—excuse me."

She laughed. "I've heard worse and I think we can agree whoever the man was, pretending to be you, he deserves that description and more."

Jesse admired that. She had her pride, but she was also willing to look at a situation and see it for what it was, not what she'd like it to be.

"Well," Will said, "my mom would have a fit if she heard me cussing in front of a lady, so excuse me anyway."

She nodded.

"As I was saying, the man who stole my identity stole more than my name. He took my reputation, too, and ran it into the ground."

Jesse scowled, seeing the look of frustration on his brother's features. He knew Will was having a hard time with all of this, but he hated seeing evidence of it.

"You didn't do anything to me," Jillian said softly.

"I know that, but as I said, it was done in my name

and I'm going to feel terrible about that unless you help me out."

A second or two passed before Jillian shook her head and smiled wryly. "Oh, you're good at this, aren't you? Getting people to do what you want, I mean."

"Used to be," Will admitted.

"Still are," Jesse said quietly.

Jillian turned her head to look at him, and their eyes locked. Even on opposite sides of the room, there was a thread of connection that snapped and crackled between them. And Jesse saw by the flash of acknowledgment in her eyes that she felt it, too. Not that he cared.

"My big brother over there knows how hard-headed I am," Will said and Jillian shifted her gaze back to him. "What I'm trying to say is, it's important to me to rebuild my good name. So let me help. If I'm worried about you and your daughter, it'll take time away from me getting back to my own life."

Jesse watched for her reaction and he could see in her eyes that she wasn't buying it. That was the only reason he spoke up when he did. "He's not lying."

She turned her head to look at him again and that electrical pulse between them erupted. Her gaze fixed on his and Jesse could have sworn even the air between them burned. He wasn't interested in this. Had no time for the distraction of a woman—and *this* woman would be the Queen of all distractions. So he pushed away any sense of attraction he was feeling and focused on making his point known. "Will's got a lot going on right now."

She laughed shortly, but her eyes remained cool and flat. "Yeah. I know."

"Then you should know he's not going to rest until you and your daughter are taken care of."

"I'm not a problem to be solved and neither is my daughter."

"He didn't mean—" Will said.

"That's not what I said," Jesse interrupted, cutting his brother off. "And I think you know it. So don't go looking to be offended when there's no intent."

Will fired a hard look at him that Jesse ignored. He never took his gaze off Jillian, so he recognized when she accepted his words.

She nodded briefly. "Okay, you're right. I was doing that."

"I'm also right about you letting Will off the hook—"

"He's not *on* a hook," Jillian snapped. "I just said so."

"I never thought I was—"

Jesse cut Will off again. "There you go. Offense where none's meant. I'm trying to tell you that if you don't let Will do what he thinks is fair and right here, you're going to punish him for something that wasn't his fault."

"Jesse, why don't you let me—"

"I told him it's not his fault," Jillian argued, and this time *she* cut Will off.

"He won't believe you," Jesse said.

"Yes, I would."

"Well, he should," Jillian said.

"He won't." Jesse waved one hand at his brother. "He'll wallow in guilt or some other nonsense if you don't let him help."

"I don't wallow," Will pointed out.

"And if I let him help," Jillian countered, "then I feel guilty for taking advantage of a man who owes me nothing."

"No, you won't," Jesse said, shaking his head. "You're too smart for that. You're a mother. You have your kid to think of. So you'll do the smart thing and take a helping hand when it's offered."

She tipped her head to study him. "Oh, will I?"

Her long, blond ponytail swung forward to lie over her shoulder and across her breast. His hands itched to do the same. Hell. He was jealous of her *hair*. How sad was that?

"Yeah," Jesse said, his gaze locked with hers. "You will."

"You two just let me know when it's my turn to talk," Will muttered.

"He's not going to let this go until you let him help," Jesse said.

"He's right about that anyway," Will broke in, grabbing his chance to get a few words in.

"Why do you care what I do or don't?" Jillian asked, but the question was for Jesse, not Will.

Truthfully, he wasn't entirely sure why her welfare mattered to him one way or the other. He shrugged. "Maybe it's because my mom was a single mother when she married Will's daddy. Because I remember how hard it was for her before we came to live here at the ranch."

Her gaze lowered briefly before she looked at him again. In her eyes, he saw acceptance. She gave him an almost imperceptible nod before looking at Will. "Okay, then. I'll take your help and thank you for it."

Will smiled. "You don't have to thank me. Like my brother said, you're helping me out of a sea of guilt just by saying yes."

Jesse watched her and knew she was still a little uneasy with her decision, but for her daughter's sake, she was clearly willing to swallow a bit of her pride.

"You were living and working in Vegas," Will said. "Is that right?"

Jillian's shoulders squared and her spine snapped straight as a plank. As if just the word *Vegas* invited judgment that she was prepared to defend herself against. "That's right."

"I can send you back there," Will was saying, "You probably gave up your apartment when you came to Texas, so I could help you get a new one, if you like. Or if you prefer, I'll find you a nice place here in Royal."

She chewed at her bottom lip and Jesse's groin went rock-hard in a flash of heat. Damn.

"I'd rather stay here in Royal," Jillian finally said, then added, "if you don't mind any gossip that might spring up. People will know why I came here—thinking you were Mackenzie's father and all."

"Doesn't bother me," Will assured her. "There's always gossip about one thing or another and it'll fade. But this is up to you. Are you sure you wouldn't rather go home?"

Now a sad smile briefly curved her wide, fantastic mouth. "Vegas was never *home.* Just a place to live and work. I came here for a fresh start. For Mac and for me. I'd still like that."

"Then that's what we'll do," Will said, and walked back around to the chair behind the desk. "We own a lot of property in Royal. I'm sure we've got an apartment—"

"It doesn't have to be anything big. Or fancy," Jillian added quickly. "Just clean and safe. Somewhere we can be until I find a job and get a place of my own."

"But—"

Will was going to argue, but Jesse knew what the woman meant. She was willing to take help but didn't want to feel beholden as she would if Will tried to give her some extravagant apartment.

"There's a place off Main." Both Will and Jillian looked at him. "Good building. Safe. Clean. They're studio apartments, but big enough for you and a baby."

Relief shone in her eyes and she nodded even as Will sputtered, "We can do better than a studio. A place with more room. A yard, maybe—"

"No." Jillian shook her head, looked at Will and said, "This one sounds perfect. We'll take it." Then she turned her gaze back to Jesse. She looked at him for a long moment, then said simply, "Thank you."

Those eyes of hers met his steadily, and he felt that swift tug of something hot again. He didn't let her know that, though. "You're welcome."

"How'd it go?"

Jillian walked into the large, plush living room of Lucy Navarro Bradshaw's suite at the Ace In the Hole ranch. The room was huge and airy, with floor-to-ceiling windows along the front wall, displaying a wide view of the ranch the Sanders family called home. The furniture was feminine without being frilly. Overstuffed couches and chairs covered in cream fabric splashed with blue and yellow flowers. Heavy, pale oak tables held stacks of books and brass lamps with amber shades. Rugs in pale, subtle colors dotted the gleaming wood floors and to make it all seem less like a photo shoot layout, toys, trucks and coloring books were scattered everywhere.

Ordinarily, Jillian would have felt completely out of place in such an elegant, old-money kind of home. But Lucy made the difference here.

At five feet six inches, Lucy was much shorter

than Jillian's five foot ten. She had layered brown hair, big blue eyes and a friendly smile that had welcomed Jillian from the first. Thanks to Lucy, even with everything that had been going on for the last two weeks, Jillian hadn't felt so *alone* in Royal.

She didn't know why Lucy had befriended her, but she was grateful. Jillian had left behind everything she'd ever known when she came to Royal, Texas, hoping for some sort of settlement from the estate of the man she'd thought was her baby girl's father. Will Sanders. It wasn't until the service for Will, when the man himself had walked through the door, that Jillian had realized she'd been duped. A damn impostor, posing as the rich, successful Will Sanders, had gotten past Jillian's defenses and left her pregnant. Now she had no home, no job, very little money and a daughter to provide for.

Thinking of her little girl had Jillian's gaze sliding to Baby Mac, playing with Lucy's son, Brody. The tiny girl had soft blond hair, big hazel eyes and a dimple in her right cheek that never failed to tug at Jillian's heart. Mackenzie Norris, closing in on two years old, and the light of her mommy's life.

There was *nothing* Jillian wouldn't do for her daughter.

"Jillian?" Lucy asked. "Earth to Jillian..."

"What?" She gave herself a shake and smiled a little. "Sorry. Mental wandering."

"Don't worry. Happens to me all the time," Lucy assured her.

"Mommy!" Mac's face lit up. "I color."

"I can see that," Jillian said, taking a spot on the floor beside Lucy and her son, the small, sandy-haired boy with eyes the color of root beer.

Brody, in his four-year-old wisdom, tried to whisper, "She goes outside the lines."

Lucy laughed and skimmed one hand down her son's head. "She's still little."

Yes, that was the reason, Jillian thought, but a part of her hoped that Mac *always* went outside the lines. She wanted her little girl to push envelopes, to reach for stars and every other heartwarming cliché on the books.

"Why don't you take Mac to your room and show her your books," Lucy suggested.

"Okay." Brody stood up and held one hand down to the toddler already scrambling to go with him.

When the kids were out of the room, Lucy gathered up the crayons and tucked them into a wide, plastic box. "So," she asked, slanting Jillian a look. "How'd it go?"

Jillian gathered up the coloring books, stacked them neatly, then laid them down beside the box of colors. "Pretty well, all things considered."

"That's called answering without answering," Lucy chided. "My mom used to do it all the time to us. Now I do it to Brody."

Jillian laughed a little. "You're right. Sorry."

"What did Will have to say?"

"Everything," she said after a second or two. Jillian thought back over their meeting and couldn't fault the man at all. He'd been kind, understanding and generous, considering that Jillian and Mac weren't his problem to deal with at all. Sighing, she leaned back against the closest chair and stretched her legs out in front of her. "He's a really nice man. Much nicer than the 'Will' I knew."

Lucy reached out and took her hand, giving it a squeeze of solidarity. "He's a good guy."

"Yeah," Jillian agreed. "He is. He offered to pay our way home to Vegas and set us up in a new apartment."

"Oh." One word of disappointment.

She glanced at Lucy and the other woman shrugged.

"I was sort of hoping you'd stay here in Texas," Lucy said. "I mean, I don't have that many close friends and, well, we just clicked, you know? So I'd miss you."

Surprised as much by Lucy as she had been by the woman's brother, Jillian asked, "Why?"

A short laugh shot from Lucy's throat. "Well, come on. Do you have so many friends that you wouldn't miss one if they moved away?"

"No," Jillian said after a moment or two. "I don't. I'd miss you, too."

"Glad to hear it," Lucy admitted.

"But I won't have to miss you."

"What?" Lucy asked. "What do you mean?"

"I'm not leaving Texas," Jillian said, then shrugged when the other woman gave her a grin. "There's nothing to go back to in Vegas and I think maybe Royal is a good place to get a fresh start."

"It's a terrific place," Lucy agreed, leaning over to give her a one-armed hug. "I'm so glad you're staying. But *where* are you staying?" She paused, then brightened. "Oh. You and Mac could move into the east wing here with me and Brody. This place is huge—there's more than enough room. Brody would love having his new friend here and frankly," she added, "so would I."

Tempting. Jillian hadn't had a friend like Lucy in well...*ever.* For some reason, the two of them had clicked almost from the start and Brody and Mac had already formed a strong friendship, too.

But staying here on Will Sanders's ranch would just be way too awkward.

Besides, Jesse would be here, too.

And she didn't think it was a good idea to spend too much time around that particular man. He made her want things she had no business wanting.

Two

Jillian took a deep breath and realized that not even Will Sanders had made her feel so jumpy and excited and eager all at once. No, she amended silently, *not* Will. Impostor Will. Back then, the impostor had swept her off her feet so fast that Jillian had forgotten all about protecting herself.

And now that she had not only herself but Mac to worry about, Jillian had to be more careful than ever. Especially since Jesse made her want to *not* be.

"Thank you," she said. "Really, thank you for offering, but we can't stay here. It would be...weird, with Will here and—"

"Okay," Lucy replied, "I get that. But you can't stay in the motel forever, either."

"We're not going to." Jillian pushed a strand of hair back from her face and tucked it behind her ear. "You and Brody have been so nice. He's so good to Mac..."

Lucy sighed a little. "He's got his daddy's disposition, thank goodness."

"I don't know, I think his mom's pretty great, too."

Lucy grinned. "But she's got a terrible temper."

Jillian laughed. "All the best of us do."

From Brody's room came the sound of laughter and the high-pitched whistle of a toy train. Jillian gave a little sigh. Brody had completely taken Mac under his very tiny wing. Only four years old himself, Jillian had the impression that he liked being the "big" kid in the eyes of nearly two-year-old Mac.

Jillian knew she was doing the right thing, staying here in Texas. Mac was happy, even in that crappy little motel they'd been staying in. There were parks to play in, ice cream shops to get treats from and there was Brody. It would work out, she told herself. She'd make sure of it.

"What are you thinking?" Lucy asked. "I can practically hear the wheels in your brain turning from here."

Jillian leaned back against the couch next to her friend. Her *friend.* And wasn't that a gift? She'd come to Texas hoping to get a settlement that would take care of her daughter only to have that dream ripped away from her. But she'd also found a good friend and a place to start over and that made up for a lot.

"Your brother—"

"Which one?" Lucy interrupted.

"Jesse," Jillian said. "He's found a place for Mac and I—" There was nothing in Vegas for her. She had no family except for Mac. No ties to that neon city and no real job prospects beyond being a cocktail waitress in one of the casinos. It was a good job and the pay wasn't terrible, but spending hours a night walking around in high heels delivering drinks to people who'd already had enough wasn't exactly her dream job. Besides, she had to have a babysitter for Mac and Jillian was starting to resent missing so much time with her little girl.

"That's great, I'm so glad."

"Me, too." She sat back on the overstuffed couch. "It'll be great to get out of that motel. Anyway, Will and I were talking and then Jesse walked in and—"

"Really?" Lucy scowled a little. "I thought Will wanted to talk to you alone. If I'd known it was a free-for-all, I'd have been downstairs, too."

"I get the feeling Jesse wasn't invited," Jillian told her. "He just…came."

Lucy nodded. "Sounds like him. What did he have to say?"

"He told me about an apartment just outside town. It's a small studio—"

"No way." Shaking her head, Lucy said, "Will can do better than that."

Jillian stopped her cold. It had been hard enough for her to accept any help at all. The thought of Will setting her and Mac up in some luxury apartment was just too much. She didn't want charity. She wanted a chance.

Glancing around the quietly beautiful room she sat in now, she acknowledged that a studio wasn't going to be anything like this, but that was okay, too. She was accustomed to making do and as long as she could find a job, save some more money, Jillian would be happy. She had plans and Royal seemed like as good a place as any to work on making those plans a reality.

"I don't want him to do better," Jillian said. "I can take care of myself and Mac. All I need is a place to start. Well, and a job."

"I can understand that, about the apartment I mean," Lucy said. "And as for the job, I might know of something if you're interested."

Surprised, Jillian fixed her gaze on her friend. "I'm interested."

Lucy laughed. "I haven't even told you what it is yet."

Kicking her long legs out in front of her, Jillian crossed her feet at the ankle. "Is it walking around in high heels wearing a Valkyrie outfit listening to drunken come-ons all night?"

"Sorry, nothing so exotic." Lucy grinned. "But now I want to see the Valkyrie outfit."

Jillian rolled her eyes. "I'd be happy to never see it again. So, what's the job?"

Shifting, Lucy pushed the stack of coloring books out of her way, then sat up cross-legged. "Okay, now understand, you don't have to take it or anything, this is just an idea. But I think it could work and you could be with Mac at the same time and—"

Jillian's lips twitched. "Just say it, Lucy."

"Okay," she pushed her dark hair back from her face, tucking it behind her ears. "They need help in the day care at the Texas Cattlemen's Club."

"Day care?" Jillian repeated, her mind already working through possibilities.

Lucy immediately started trying to convince her. "It's really a great place, just a few years old, actually. Brody's been there a few times, when I've got clients to see and Mom's not available. But the thing is, Mac could be there when you're working. She can make friends, and you wouldn't have to worry about her and—"

Jillian held up one hand and laughed. "I don't need the sales pitch. It's a great idea."

"Fantastic," Lucy cried. "From what I hear, the pay's not bad and you wouldn't have to get a babysitter, since Mac could be with you, so you'd actually be making more money. I've already told Ginger Hanks all about you and she's excited to meet you. I thought if it's okay with you, we could go down there tomorrow. I'll introduce you and you can check the place out and see if you'll like it or not."

"Thank you." Jillian grabbed the other woman's hand and squeezed. "I really appreciate this, Lucy."

"Completely self-serving," she said, squeezing back. "I didn't want to lose you to Vegas."

She snorted. "No chance of that."

"Good. I'll find out where this apartment is from Will and take you by there tomorrow, too, if you want..."

"Not necessary."

Jillian's heart jumped into a gallop at the sound. That voice was so deep it seemed to roll through the room, demanding attention. Slowly, she slanted a look at the man standing in the open doorway. *What* was it about cowboys?

Just by looking at him, she could tell that Jesse Navarro was the kind of man who walked into a room and all eyes turned to him. Men wanted to be him and women just *wanted* him. Jillian had seen his type before, but Jesse took it to a whole new level. She'd never run into a man who simply *breathed* confidence and strength. It was a little unsettling, especially when you yourself were feeling just a little off balance anyway.

In a couple of quick seconds, her gaze swept him

up and down and as she did, her heartbeat did a fluttery thing that she had zero business experiencing.

He just stood there, watching her. His eyes were like melted chocolate, his dark brown hair curled over the collar of his long-sleeved white shirt. The hem of faded black jeans stacked on the tops of his scuffed black boots and he held his black cowboy hat in one hand at his side. So still, she thought, and somehow *powerful* in that stillness. Enough that her heart did another wild series of beats that hammered in her ears and made her breathing just a little rough.

"Of course it's necessary, Jesse." Lucy spoke up. "It's not like Jillian knows her way around town yet."

He shifted his gaze briefly to his sister. "Lucy, you've got that meeting in the morning with the architect about your new breeding barn?"

Jillian tore her gaze from Jesse, because it was way safer to look at the other woman in the room. "Breeding barn?"

Lucy waved one hand. "Jesse likes to call it that. But I am building a new stable for the horses I'm—"

"Breeding?" Jesse asked.

"Fine. Yes. A breeding barn." She blew out a breath. "And he's right. I forgot about the meeting. Okay then, Jesse will take you to the apartment tomorrow and then I'll take you over to the TCC so you can find out about the job."

Jillian felt like she was being pushed downhill. She wanted to stop but she had the feeling the only way that was going to happen now was if she ran into a tree. Still, she had to try.

"Thank you," she said to Jesse, "but I've got GPS on my phone, so you really don't have to take me—"

"It's decided," he said, then gave both women a sharp nod. "I'll pick you up at your motel about ten, that all right?"

"Pointless to argue with him," Lucy gave a dramatic sigh. "He's got a head like solid concrete."

Jesse frowned at her, but there was no anger in the look, Jillian noted. Just brother-sister stuff, which was sort of entertaining to see. If she hadn't been right in the middle of it.

"If you'll just give me the address," she tried again.

"I will. Once we get there," Jesse told her. "See you then."

When he left, Jillian took a deep breath and let it slowly out again. "Your brother is—"

"Pushy? Opinionated? Arrogant?" Lucy provided with a grin. "My answer is D. All of the above."

And don't forget dangerously sexy.

Jillian swallowed hard. "Does anyone ever say no to him?"

"Many have tried, few have succeeded," Lucy admitted wryly. "You're okay with him taking you tomorrow, aren't you? I mean, he really is a good guy." She paused, gave Jillian a sly smile. "And he's single."

Jillian blinked. She'd seen that gleam in the eyes of other friends over the years and she knew that Lucy was trying her hand at a little matchmaking. Which just was not going to happen.

The whole setup thing always turned into a nightmare. Besides, she wasn't looking for a man. The last one she'd found had been the impostor who had swept her off her feet then left her pregnant and wondering who the heck her baby's father really was. No, she'd had enough of men. What she wanted now was to build a home for her baby girl. She wanted to make a future for the two of them and a man was a distraction she didn't want or need.

"No thanks," Jillian finally said, pushing up from the floor. Outside, the afternoon was slipping away and soon, a spectacular sunset would be staining the sky. "I'm not looking for a man. And I'm *really* not looking for one who likes to tell people what to do."

"Oh, he's not that bad. He's not a bully or anything, he's just…Jesse." Lucy shrugged and stood up, too.

"Uh-huh. And was your husband bossy?" The instant the words were out, Jillian wanted to drag them back into her mouth and lock her lips closed. Since she couldn't, she said, "I'm so sorry. I shouldn't have mentioned—"

"Relax," Lucy soothed, reaching out to give Jillian a quick hug. "I'm the one who told you I'm a widow, remember? I don't mind talking about Dane. I want

Brody to hear about his daddy, so those of us who knew him *have* to talk about him."

Didn't make Jillian feel any better.

"But to answer your question, no, he wasn't bossy. After hanging around with Jesse and Will for a while, he tried to be, but he just couldn't pull it off." Lucy laughed a little in memory. "Dane was nothing like Jesse, really. Or Will, for that matter. But to be fair to my oldest brother, he's so used to taking charge I don't think it ever occurs to him to *not* do it, you know?"

No, she really didn't. Not one man Jillian had ever known had been the responsible type. They didn't want to take charge because they hadn't wanted to be blamed if things went wrong. Heck, her own father had walked out on his family when Jillian was just five because he hadn't wanted the responsibility of a family. So she didn't have any experience with men like Jesse. And maybe, she told herself, that was why he was bothering her so much. She couldn't pigeonhole him into any of the types she was most familiar with.

And maybe that was a good thing, since being a cocktail waitress in a casino gave her an up close and personal look at the worst kind of men. The takers. The whiners. The braggers. Now thanks to the impostor who'd convinced her he was crazy about her, she had another category. The liars. So far, Jesse Navarro seemed to be in a category all to himself.

"Well," she finally said, "I take care of myself and Mac and I don't take orders well."

"Then this should be interesting," Lucy murmured, and Jillian was pretty sure her friend was amused by the whole situation.

The apartment was clean.

That was the best Jesse could say about it the following morning. Hell, when he'd first suggested this place, he'd remembered the apartments being better than this. Bigger. Less...*institutional.* With Jillian and her daughter at his side, Jesse felt like apologizing for suggesting this apartment in the first place.

"It's perfect." Jillian walked farther into the numbingly boring, impersonal space.

"Put your glasses on," he muttered.

She whipped around to look at him. "I don't wear glasses. I see it clearly enough and this will be fine. It's got a lot of windows, so it's nice and bright."

"Which just makes me wonder why you're not seeing what I am when I look at this place. It's like a prison cell," he added, letting his gaze slide around the one big room.

At one end, there was a small, but complete kitchen, with a fridge, microwave, stove and dishwasher. The countertop was serviceable black, the cabinets were painted white and the sink was stainless steel. On the opposite side of the room was a double bed and against the front wall was a couch with a chair pulled up alongside and a tiny coffee table in front of it. There was a small bathroom with a tub/shower off the main room and he guessed the other doors were for the closet. Which pretty much described the whole place.

A beige, claustrophobic closet.

"Know a lot about prison cells, do you?" she asked.

He shot her a quick look. "Not personally, but I've seen movies. This would make a good set for one of them."

"There's nothing wrong with it," she argued. "A little paint, a few rugs and a bright quilt will make it shine."

"Shine?" he repeated dubiously. He walked toward the kitchen—took him four steps—and turned around at the sound of bedsprings squeaking. Mac was jumping up and down on the mattress, a gleeful look on her little face. Leave it to a kid. Even in a cell, they'd find a way to have fun.

"Mac, baby," Jillian cooed, "don't jump on the bed…"

"Might fall apart," Jesse muttered, scowling as he looked around the room again.

Jillian scooped Mac up in her arms, then turned to face him. "It's perfectly fine for us."

"The whole place could fit inside my living room." He shoved both hands into his jeans pockets.

She flushed at that and said, "Not all of us need that much room."

"Not all of us want to live in a box, either," he countered.

"Really?" She tipped her head to one side and stared at him. "This was your idea, remember?"

"Don't remind me," he muttered darkly. When he got back to the ranch, he was going to talk to Will about this building. Get someone in here, a designer or something to make these places less…depressing.

His gaze fixed on the woman watching him. Today, she wore yoga pants that looked as though they'd been painted onto her long, long legs and defined a figure he'd only guessed at before. She had a dancer's body, he thought, slim, but curvy in all the right places. The long-sleeved red shirt she wore over those black pants strained across breasts he'd really like to get his hands on and that tail of wavy blond hair hung over one shoulder as if drawing an arrow he didn't need to the breasts he was thinking too much about. Her hazel eyes were more green than blue today and he wondered what that said about her mood.

"Jesse!" Mac leaned out from her mother's grasp and held both arms out to him.

Dutifully, he stepped forward and plucked the girl off her mother's hip.

"You don't have to hold her," Jillian said, as if apologizing for her daughter.

"If I had to, I wouldn't want to," he said, and turned to look at the little girl clinging to him. She tugged at him, as completely as Brody did. But with Mac, he didn't feel the twin tug of guilt that he did with his nephew. "What do you think, Mac? You want to stay here or go back to the ranch?"

"Horsies!"

Grimly, he nodded. "That settles it. You can stay at the ranch until you find a better place. There's plenty of room there and—"

"No," Jillian told him.

"Excuse me?"

"Don't hear that word often, do you?" she asked. "Well, you'll have to deal with it. Mac isn't even two yet. Of course she wants to be with the horses, but she's not the one making decisions for our family. We'll be staying right here."

He saw the stubborn glint in her eyes and knew she'd dig her heels in on this, so he let it go. For now. But the damn truth was, she and Mac could stay at the ranch with no problem. There was the main house, his mother's cabin, a couple guest cottages... more than enough room for one woman and a tiny girl, and if they were there, Jesse wouldn't have to feel like he'd dropped them off in a dump.

"It's not a dump," she said, and he blinked. Had he said that last part aloud?

"You're not that hard to read," Jillian explained.

That made him frown. No man liked to be told he was clear as glass, and Jesse more than most had always prided himself on his poker face. Unless he wanted them to, no one knew what he was thinking. Well, until today.

"Dump!" Mac cried, clapping her hands.

He laughed shortly. "She agrees with me."

"Again," Jillian pointed out. "She's a baby." Then, turning around, she plopped both hands on her hips and gave the whole apartment a thorough look-see. Took her about ten seconds.

"I'll get a couple of rugs, but the hardwood floors are gorgeous."

"Not very big," he said.

"I'll paint the walls a pretty green, I think…"

"Won't need much."

"I'll get a crib for Mac and put it at the foot of the bed…"

"Don't get a big one."

She inhaled and sighed heavily, ignoring him. "Maybe a little table and two chairs…"

"*Very* little table."

"You know," she said, suddenly spinning around to face him, fire in her eyes and battle on her features. "You're not being helpful."

"I'm not trying to be," he said flatly. "This isn't much bigger than that motel you and Mac have been staying at."

"It's big enough. I'll get that job, take my time, look around and find something else when I'm ready."

"You should be ready now," he argued.

"I don't take orders from you."

"I'm not giving you an order. If I were, you'd follow it."

"Is that right?" She actually laughed and if he hadn't been so irritated, he'd have been charmed. That deep voice of hers sounded even sexier when she was laughing. Her eyes lit up and that incredible mouth of hers moved into a smile that was too damn seductive.

"You think a lot of yourself," she said, "but nobody tells me what to do."

"Somebody should," he countered, then huffed out an exasperated breath. "Look, I suggested this place, but now that I'm seeing it again, it's just not right. You and Mac, you deserve better."

Irritation slid off her face and she gave him another smile. This one warmer than the last. "Thank you. And you're right. We do. But I'm the one who's going to get it for us."

Hard to argue with pride since he had plenty of that himself. "Can't talk you out of this?"

She spun around again, taking another all-too-brief look. When she met his gaze, she said, "Nope. But you could drive us to the motel and help me move our things over here."

"Yeah," he said tightly. "Guess I could do that."

"Jesse! Horsies?" Mac asked, cupping her little hands on his cheeks to turn his eyes to her.

"Not right now, sweet girl," he said and frowned at the disappointment in the tiny girl's eyes.

Over the last couple of weeks, Mac and her mother had been at the ranch several times, and each time they were, the little girl had demanded time with the horses. He'd taken her up for her first ride himself and she hadn't been able to get enough. He knew what that felt like. He'd been about six the first time Roy Sanders had set him on a horse, and Jesse had known in that moment that he'd found where he belonged. Now little Mac had fallen for the same animals that had stolen Jesse's heart so many years ago.

So he tugged a lock of her hair gently and said, "We'll see the horses later, okay?"

"You shouldn't promise her something you might not be able to deliver on," Jillian warned. "She doesn't forget a thing."

He slanted his gaze to hers and locked on like a targeting system. "I always keep my promises."

Her eyes said she didn't believe him, and Jesse wondered what had made her so distrustful. Of course, the minute that thought entered his mind, he remembered why she was in Royal in the first place. A man had lied to her, used her and left her pregnant and alone. The kind of man who did that was no man at all to Jesse's way of thinking. And if he ever found the bastard, he'd make sure the son of a bitch paid for the pain he'd put so many people through.

But was it just the impostor who'd put that wary look in Jillian's eyes? Or was it more? And why did he give a flying damn?

He didn't.

"Come on," he said abruptly. "I'll take you back to the motel. We'll get your stuff."

"Stuff!" Mac laughed at the new word, and Jillian smiled.

Jesse met her eyes and he watched as her smile faded. Probably best, he told himself. If that mouth of hers kept curving so temptingly, he wouldn't be able to resist tasting it.

And then where would they be?

Three

The Texas Cattleman's Club was impressive. A large, rambling single-story building, it was built from dark wood and stone, and had a tall slate roof. It looked just as a Texas men's club should look, Jillian thought. Historically, the TCC had been a rich man's private retreat. But all of that started changing several years ago, according to Lucy. Women became members, then took positions on the board and slowly but surely began to drag the TCC into the twenty-first century—with, no doubt, its oldest members kicking and screaming the whole way.

But Jillian could understand why the men had

fought to hold on to one of their last bastions. Yes, she was a feminist. But there were times she wanted to be around only women. So why wouldn't men want the same thing occasionally?

Still, their loss was definitely her gain. One of the first things the female members of the club did was to open a day care center at the club. It was just to the left of the entrance in what had once been a billiards room. There were lots of windows and a set of French doors that opened out onto a shaded grassy area where the kids could play. The walls were white, but dotted with artwork provided by the children who spent the days there.

There were tiny tables and chairs and rugs in bright primary colors. Pint-sized easels were arranged on one side of the room where kids could paint and draw. Shelves filled with books and toys were neatly arranged along one wall. There was a small half kitchen with a fridge, a sink and a microwave that came in handy for preparing snacks and meals for the kids.

Ginger Hanks, about fifty with graying red hair, bright blue eyes and a knowing smile, was the manager, and there were two other women employed there, as well. If she got the job, Jillian would be the third helper, and as she was shown around, she realized she really did want the job.

She'd always loved kids, and being able to have

her little girl with her while she was at work was a bonus she couldn't even imagine.

"The number of children we have every day differs," Ginger was saying as she led Lucy and Jillian around the room, taking a tour. "Sometimes it's twenty, other days it's five or six. Members of the club are welcome to leave their kids here while they use the facilities, or even if they're going out to lunch or shopping or something. We also have a few children who are here every day while their parents work."

"It's a great place," Jillian said and earned a wide smile of approval from Ginger.

"Thank you, we think so." Ginger bent down to scoop up a crying baby from one of the cribs pushed against the wall. The instant she did, the infant stopped crying. "Of course, you have to love children to work here."

"Oh, I do. I have a nearly two-year-old myself," she said and half wished she'd brought Mac with her. But a job interview hadn't seemed the right time to bring her daughter, so she'd left Mac at the Sanders ranch with Lucy's mother.

"Lucy told me, and you're welcome to bring her to work with you." Ginger looked around at the kids coloring, doing their numbers and letters, playing with dolls or trains.

"I told you," Lucy said, nudging Jillian.

"That's a relief to me." Jillian held out her hands toward Ginger and asked, "May I?"

The older woman gave her a long look before nodding and handing the baby over. Jillian cuddled the baby boy close and began an instinctive side-to-side sway. Ginger gave another approving smile.

"You've got a way with little ones, don't you?"

"Oh, I love babies," Jillian admitted. "I used to think I'd have a houseful of my own."

"You've got plenty of time for more babies."

Yes, she did. But she didn't have a man in her life and since that wasn't going to be changing anytime soon, Jillian could admit to herself that Mac would most likely be an only child. Just as she had been. The difference was, Jillian would make sure her little girl never felt as though she weren't important. Mac would never know what it was like to listen to her parents shout at each other. Never know what it was to have those parents walk away from her without a backward glance. She would never have to doubt that she was loved.

Sighing a little, she told herself she could indulge her love for babies right here—if she got the job.

"That's little Danny Moses, isn't it?" Lucy asked, taking a peek at the baby's face.

"Sure is," Ginger confirmed. "He's good as gold, too. His mama's out on a lunch date with his daddy, so we're keeping him happy here."

Jillian's heart hurt a little as she held the baby and

looked down into that tiny face. Days were going by so quickly it could make her head spin sometimes. It seemed like just yesterday Mac was this size and now she was talking and walking, and Jillian knew she had no time to lose—it was time to build that future she'd dreamed of.

"I'm glad Lucy brought you here today," Ginger said thoughtfully.

"Oh, so am I," Jillian told her, flashing a smile. "I don't want to put you on the spot or anything but I really would love to work here."

"That's plain to see," Ginger assured her and took the baby from Jillian. "I've got another woman coming in for an interview later this afternoon. Once that's done, I'll be in touch soon."

Jillian forced a smile, though she wanted to say, *Don't meet anyone else, hire me*. "Thank you."

When they turned to go, Jillian didn't see Ginger give Lucy a wink and a thumbs-up.

All right, Jesse kept his promise.

Jillian leaned on the corral fence and watched her daughter sitting atop what looked like a *gigantic* horse. The afternoon sun was bright, but the air was already warm. Early summer in Texas wasn't that different from Vegas weather. Of course, that was where the similarities ended.

In Las Vegas, the city was bright, crowded, noisy and jammed with locals and tourists. There was never a quiet moment unless you left the city and then you were in the middle of a desert, with no shade, no water, no trees. No nothing.

Here, though, there were oak trees, rivers, lakes, and there was quiet when you wanted it and plenty of noise to be found when you didn't. People were friendlier, less cynical. Jillian already knew more people in Royal after two weeks than she had known in Vegas after five years of living there. It was a different sort of feeling in small-town Texas and it was just what she wanted for her daughter. Mac would grow up in a place where people would know her, look out for her. She'd have friends and a home and a mother who would always be there for her.

It had been a big day so far. A new apartment—that would be fine once she fixed it up—and a job interview that she really hoped would work out. And now, she was back on a ranch staring at a cowboy who turned her insides to mush. Jillian's thoughts dissolved when a delighted squeal pierced the air. She fixed her gaze on the big man walking beside her baby and that horse. Jesse had one strong hand on her little girl's back, steadying her, while he held the horse's reins in the other hand, keeping the animal just as steady, Jillian hoped.

"Don't be worried. My kids are all great with horses."

Jillian turned to watch Cora Lee Sanders walk up to join her at the fence. In her sixties, Cora Lee was about five feet three inches tall, had thick, wavy, shoulder-length gray hair and sharp, grayish green eyes. Today she wore dark blue jeans, a yellow shirt beneath a black jacket and black flats. She also boasted a silver belt buckle at her waist that glinted in the afternoon sun. Cora Lee was every inch a matriarch. There were lines in her face, of course, but they were etched there by laughter, tears and years of living that had made her the woman she was today.

"It just makes me nervous," Jillian admitted. "That horse is so big compared to Mac."

Cora Lee smiled, laid her forearms on the top rail of the fence and watched her son walk slowly around the corral. "I can understand that. As mothers, we all will do whatever it is we have to to watch out for our children."

"True." She looked at Cora Lee and saw a woman who'd been through her own trials and had triumphed. Just as Jillian planned to.

"But in this case," the older woman said, "worry is unnecessary. That horse? That's Ivy. Sweet mare. She was one of Lucy's first rescues. Would you believe when the vet first brought her here, you could count her rib bones, poor thing. Someone tied her up in a barn and then moved, never telling anyone Ivy was there." Cora Lee's mouth turned into a tight frown. "If it hadn't been for one of the Stillwell boys cutting across the property taking a shortcut home from school and hearing her, she'd have died there, too."

"That's terrible."

"It really was. Nothing on this earth should be treated with such vicious neglect. But with a lot of love and good food and time, she's healthy now and even pregnant for the first time."

Jillian smiled, looking at the horse with new admiration. Ivy hadn't let her past get in the way, either.

"She's the most gentle animal on the face of the planet. And lazy with it, if truth be told. Likes nothing better than standing still under a shade tree and avoids running as if it would kill her."

Jillian's lips twitched. "Well, that's good then."

Cora gave her a quick look. "And not only that, but Jesse's a good hand with children. Patience. He got that from his father, not me."

Glancing at the woman beside her, Jillian waited, sure there was more. She wasn't disappointed.

"His biological father, I mean. That was the most patient man on the face of the planet." She chuckled, then added, "Now, Roy Sanders, the man who raised Jesse and Lucy and was their father in every possible way, was as impatient as I am." She laughed a little harder, gave a sigh and shook her head. "It's a wonder the two of us got along at all. But my, we had some good times. Some wonderful fights, too."

"Wonderful fights?" Even Jillian could hear the doubt in her voice. But she had too many memories of her own parents before they'd abandoned her, indulging in shouting matches that had terrified her.

"If you're arguing with the right man, yes." Resting her chin on her hands, Cora Lee said, "My own mother used to say, don't fight in front of your children. But Roy and I figured that wasn't healthy, either. Children grow up expecting everything to be sunshine and roses all the time and then they're never happy. But your kids see you arguing, then see you hugging and making up, they know you can disagree without the world crashing."

Jillian smiled. "I never thought of it like that, but I think you have a point."

Nodding, the older woman said, "You kids today don't know how much good a clearing-the-air fight can do for a marriage. Keeps things hopping, that's for sure."

The only fights Jillian had experienced were blurry memories of raised voices, tears and drama, with one or the other of her parents vowing to leave and never come back. There'd never been any hugging and making up. Maybe if there had been her parents wouldn't have left.

"There you are, Mom," Lucy called as she and Brody walked up to the fence to join the party. "We went to your cottage because Brody said you'd have cookies."

"You bet I do," Cora Lee said, scooping her grandson up onto her hip. "Who's my favorite four-year-old in the whole world?"

"I am!" Brody shouted and threw his arms around his grandmother's neck.

"Displaced by Grandma and her cookies," Lucy mused.

"Must be nice," Jillian said without really thinking about it, "to have your whole family right here on the ranch."

"Oh, it is," Lucy agreed. "But thank God we don't all live in the same house."

"Thank God," Brody parroted.

"That's enough of that, little man," Cora warned and shot her daughter a hard look.

Lucy just grinned. She pointed to where a small, English-style cottage sat amid a stand of oak trees. It had dormer windows, a stone chimney and a bright red door behind the snowy white porch railings. Roses, dormant now, climbed a trellised arch just in front of the porch.

"That's Mom's place. She moved in there once we were grown, said the big house should belong to Will."

"It was only right," Cora Lee said. "Time for my kids to build their own lives and they didn't need their mama watching their every move."

"There wasn't any point trying to talk her out of it, either." Lucy nodded and swung around to point toward another house not far away. "That's Jesse's place."

Jillian turned her head to study it for a long moment and decided it suited the man to a T. The building was low and long, with a stone front porch that seemed to run around the perimeter of the place. There were two stone chimneys jutting into the sky from a slate gray metal roof and a wide set of double front doors in the center. The house itself was wood and glass and managed to look masculine and cozy all at the same time. There were chairs, rockers and swings dotting that porch and she could imagine sitting there in the evening, watching a sunset. With that image came another of her and Jesse sitting on one of those swings together, and the instant she realized what her brain was up to, Jillian shut it down fast. Thankfully, no one else seemed to notice that her imagination was working against her.

"There are three guest cottages along the back of the big house," Lucy was saying, "so whoever's staying there has easy access to the pool and—"

"What's that house there?" Jillian pointed to what looked like an oversized bungalow with chimneys on each end of the house. Again, a wide front porch graced the building, but here, there was a balcony on the second floor, too.

"That was my house," Lucy admitted. "Mine and my husband's." Her voice dropped and a small sigh escaped her. "We were in the process of building it when Dane's accident happened. When he died, I just stayed at the main house. I didn't want to live there without him.

"The house was finished before I gave birth to Brody, but we never moved in. The big house works for us."

Jillian wondered if she could push her foot any further into her mouth or if even *she'd* already reached her limit. "I'm so sorry."

"Don't be," Cora Lee said, speaking up for her daughter. "Life happens whether we're ready or not, doesn't it, little man?" She turned her gaze on Brody.

"Can I have cookies?" he asked.

"You bet." Cora Lee hitched him higher on her hip and looked at her daughter. "Brody's with me." Then she added, "If you're going to be here a while, Jillian, why don't you bring Mackenzie by, too? We'll all have cookies together."

"Thank you," she replied without agreeing to anything.

When it was just she and Lucy again, Jillian said one more time, "I'm really sorry, Lucy. I didn't mean to bring up bad memories."

Lucy laid one hand on her forearm. "They're not *bad* memories at all. How could they be?" She shook her head and looked out at Jesse and the little girl squirming excitedly in the saddle.

"You said Dane had an accident?" Jillian asked

quietly, since her friend seemed willing to talk about the past that no doubt still haunted her.

"He did. I loved Dane like crazy and he was eager to be here on the ranch. Of course he didn't know anything about horses, but he wanted to learn."

Lucy stared into the corral but Jillian knew she was looking at images much further away. Her gaze was fixed on the past and the memories brought a smile to her lips and a film of tears to her eyes.

"What happened?" Jillian's voice was a whisper.

"Just a freak twist of events that Dane was caught up in," Lucy said wistfully. "Jesse loves training horses. I mean, the ranch is his now and he loves that too, the cattle, the feed crops, all of it. But horses," Lucy said on a sigh, "hold his heart. Like they do mine. Dad left me in charge of the stud program, breeding exceptional saddle horses. And I'm also taking in rescue horses. Horses that have been abused or neglected—" Her features tightened and anger shone in her eyes. "I can't stand seeing animals hurt.

"But Jesse, his specialty is training the untrainable horse. He's got a good reputation, too. People from all over Texas bring their problem horses here and he finds a way."

Jillian wanted to say something, but damned if she could think of anything that would either stop Lucy now or make it easier to go on. Instead, all she could do was stay silent, stay close.

"A man from Waco brought Jesse a stallion to break and train." Smiling, Lucy added, "That was the meanest horse I'd ever seen. Hated everybody. But Jesse knew he could tame it. Jesse asked Dane if he wanted to help and he jumped at the chance."

Jillian's eyes closed briefly as she braced herself for what must be coming.

Lucy took a deep breath and blew it out. "The horse broke free and went a little crazy. Dane rushed in to help Jesse contain the stallion—and he was trampled."

Instantly, Jillian's gaze flicked to Mac astride that horse and she wanted to run out there and grab her girl, keep her safe. Yes, irrational, but the need was there.

"Nobody's fault, really," Lucy said quietly. "The horse wasn't to blame, either. He was just mad and scared and reacted the only way he could. Dane had a lot of broken bones, spinal injuries, but it was the head injury that killed him." She rested her chin on her joined hands on the rail fence. "He was in a coma a week before I finally accepted that he was gone. They pulled the plug that afternoon and the very next day I found out I was pregnant with Brody."

"Oh, my God." Jillian slumped against the fence, heart hurting. For all the troubles she'd had in her life, nothing could compare to what Lucy had already endured. Admiration filled her, because this woman was strong enough to get past her own grief and build a life for her son. She didn't hold on to bitterness or sit in a corner and scream *Why me?* She just went on with her life, taking care of Brody and focusing on the future. Jillian understood that.

"Wow." Lucy laughed shortly and slanted Jillian an apologetic glance. "That got grim fast. Sorry. Didn't mean to unload all of that on you."

"Don't apologize." She shook her head. "One of these days, I'll tell you my own sad stories and then we'll be even."

"Deal." Lucy's smile was wide and bright.

"I'm curious though," she said, shifting her gaze back to the man in the corral. "How did that accident affect Jesse?"

"It was bad for a long time," Lucy admitted. "He blamed himself. Still does, I think, in spite of how often I tell him there's no blame to be handed out."

Jillian thought Lucy was probably right. There was a darkness in Jesse's eyes; shadows that seemed to never lift. "What happened to the horse?"

"Oh, Jesse trained him. After that day, the stallion seemed to settle down. He went home a different animal."

Of course Jesse kept training the horse. He wasn't the kind of man to walk away from a job half-done, no matter the pain that surrounded the task. Funny that Jillian felt she knew Jesse so well after knowing him such a short time.

"Anyway, different subject entirely." Lucy turned

to her and waited until Jillian was looking into her eyes to continue. "I actually came out here to tell you that I talked to Ginger at the day care—she forgot to get your cell number earlier—and she wants to know if you can start working on Monday."

Stunned, Jillian only stared at her. "Don't I have to be background-checked or...something?"

Tipping her head to one side, Lucy said softly, "Sweetie, when you showed up here claiming Will was Mac's father, every one of the Sanders lawyers went over your background with a dozen combs each."

"Oh." She swallowed hard. "Fabulous."

"I let Ginger know that everything had been checked already and that you're good." Lucy shrugged. "Told her if she had any specific questions, she should contact one of our lawyers. But the Sanders word goes a long way here."

Jillian wondered if the lawyers had enjoyed what they'd found? Silently, she ticked through her personal history. Father left the family when Jillian was a kid. Mother left two years later. Grandma Rhonda raised Jillian, taught her how to cook, instilled in her how to be loyal and strong and other lessons Rhonda's own daughter had never learned.

At nineteen, Jillian was engaged briefly to a rodeo cowboy who left because he decided he wasn't made to be a family man. Showgirl at a casino on the strip, then she met Will Sanders—or, she reminded herself, a reasonable facsimile—and he left her life without a backward glance.

Only this time, the man walking away from her had left her with something precious. Her daughter, Mac. And for that, she'd always be grateful to… whoever he was.

She wasn't a thief, had never been arrested or even gotten so much as a speeding ticket. But still, it wasn't much of a résumé.

"Stop looking so stricken." Lucy's elbow nudged Jillian's arm. "Ginger hired you, right?"

"True," she said, nodding to herself. Apparently, making bad choices and having every man you ever cared anything for walk out on you wasn't enough to keep her from getting the job. And that was what mattered, right?

If the people in Royal found out about her past, it shouldn't count at all. Because Jillian's past wasn't going to define her. It was her present she had to think about. And the future she was going to build. For herself. For Mac. And nobody was going to stop her.

"So, now that you're employed—"

And didn't that sound good?

"—let's talk about your apartment. Jesse tells me you're thinking of painting," Lucy said.

"Oh, absolutely." She grinned and sent another look at Mac, still laughing and squealing atop Ivy as Jesse walked them around the perimeter of the corral. Sighing, she added, "Beige walls are just so… boring."

"Agreed. Do you want some help?"

Jillian looked at the other woman and smiled. It was good to have a friend again. Good to feel like she was already carving a place for herself into Royal. "I really would."

"Great. Let's get Mac and hit the hardware store." Lucy's eyes were gleaming as she scrubbed her hands together in anticipation. "Oooh. Even better, we could leave Mac and Brody with Mom and not have to ride herd on kids in the paint department."

Thinking of Mac's adventurous nature and all the possibilities for getting into trouble in a hardware store gave Jillian cold chills. And yet. "Oh, I couldn't…"

"Sure you can." Lucy turned toward her brother. "Hey, Jesse, when you finish Mac's ride will you take her over to Mom's?"

"Not a problem," he said, never taking his eyes off the little girl in his charge.

That should make Jillian feel better. But leaving Mac behind with Cora again seemed like an imposition. She'd already watched Mac for a couple hours earlier today so Jillian could take the interview.

"Don't back out," Lucy said and tugged at Jillian's arm to get her moving. "If we get the paint right away, we can go by the Courtyard and check out the shops for furniture."

True, she'd have to buy a few things, anyway, but she didn't want to spend a lot of the money she had put away. Jillian had other plans for that. "No, I don't think I'll…"

"They have the cutest little consignment shop there. You'll love it. And oh, I'll look for a new desk for Brody. He's getting so big, I swear. He's going to kindergarten next year, can you believe it?" Lucy kept up a steady stream of conversation as she simply dragged Jillian in her wake all the way to a shiny red truck. Apparently, she was determined to not give Jillian a chance to change her mind.

Then she opened the passenger door and said, "Oh, when we're finished shopping, we can stop at the Sweets and Treats, bring Mom some of the fruit tarts they sell there. They're her favorite and it's the perfect way of saying thanks."

Jillian stopped dead and narrowed her eyes on Lucy. The innocence stamped on the woman's features didn't fool Jillian one bit. "That was pretty slick, telling me how to thank your mother for doing me a favor I didn't ask her to do."

Lucy's head tipped to one side and she grinned. "Wasn't it? Oh, come on. Admit it. You know you want to."

Jillian looked back over her shoulder to where her daughter was being swung up into the arms of a tall, gorgeous cowboy. Oh, what she was feeling for

Jesse was dangerous. Especially because just for a second, she was envious of her baby girl.

Not a good sign.

Leaving was definitely the right thing to do.

Four

"Jillian's a lovely girl…"

Every instinct Jesse possessed went on high alert as he shot a wary look at his mother. Cora Lee was a strong woman who'd held her family together no matter what had come at them. She'd survived the loss of two husbands and had raised her three children while single-handedly running one of the biggest ranches in Texas until he and Will had come of age to take over.

Over the years, she hadn't slowed down much, either. She didn't run the ranch or the business end of the Sanders company anymore, but she kept up with what was happening both on the ranch and in Royal.

Cora Lee wasn't a woman to sit back and watch life go by—she jumped in and did whatever the hell she wanted or needed to do. She'd never once in her life thought that being a woman somehow made her "less"—and she hadn't let anyone else believe it, either. She was strong, confident and impossible to ignore because she simply refused to allow her children to duck her interference.

She kept her fingers on the pulse of Royal, always knowing what was going on and why. Just as she somehow always seemed to know what her grown kids were up to. Jesse, Will and Lucy were her life and she didn't mind one little bit sticking her nose in if she thought any of them needed her "help."

"Yeah, she is," he said in as noncommittal a way as he could manage. Damn. Jesse'd thought that with Will back, their mother would be more focused on *him.* It seemed Cora Lee was the queen of multitasking.

"She's had a hard life," his mom mused thoughtfully.

"Imagine so." He hadn't looked at the background records the lawyers had dug up on Jillian. It had been enough for Jesse that they'd told him she'd checked out and wasn't trying to pull a fast one. Apparently, though, his mother had read the file.

Jesse took a gulp of coffee and told himself to run for it. He could take most anything and stand his ground. Hell, he'd faced flash floods and lightning storms on the open land without blinking. But when his mother started in on him, it was smarter to bolt.

Decision made, he set the screwdriver he still held down on the counter. "Thanks for the coffee. I think that cupboard door's good now, but if the hinge comes loose again, let me know."

"You're not fooling me, you know," Cora Lee said softly. "I know a grown man trying to hide from his mother when I see one."

Well, that stopped him. Shooting her a look over his shoulder, he asked wryly, "Can you really blame me?"

Cora Lee considered that for a second or two, then smiled. "I guess not. Fine. You can relax. I won't say another word about Jillian."

"Thanks."

"For now."

He rolled his eyes. Jesse was beginning to suspect there'd been nothing wrong with the damn cabinet he'd just spent fifteen minutes fixing in the first place. His mother had probably loosened the hinge so she'd have an excuse to trap him in her kitchen.

Her cottage was quiet. The kids were gone, Brody with his mother to the main house and Mac with Jillian back to their new prison cell. He scowled at the thought. Still didn't like the idea of them living in that tiny, lifeless place, but the woman was as stubborn as she was beautiful.

His mind dredged up the image of Jillian laughing

with Lucy when they came back from their spur-of-the-moment shopping trip. She'd looked…relaxed, like her guard was down, and a hot fist of need had grabbed Jesse by the balls and hadn't let go yet.

He didn't like his reactions to Jillian but hadn't been able to control them yet, either. It seemed that woman had the ability to turn him inside out just by looking at him. So, the last thing he needed was his mother's well-meant but unnecessary advice or opinion. Hell, he liked his life just fine the way it was. He wasn't looking for a family. He already *had* a family and a kid he would always be responsible for because Brody's father had died under Jesse's watch. So yeah. No changes to his life needed. When he wanted a woman he went out and got one. Drinks, dinner and sex filled out a single evening and then he was back to his real world. This ranch. His family.

What with Will coming back from the dead, Lucy a widow and Brody fatherless, he didn't need one more damn thing to think about. No more drama.

He opened the back door to leave, but stopped when his mother spoke up again. "Jesse."

The speculative, my-son-needs-a-wife gleam in her eyes had been replaced by a glimmer of the concern and worry etched into her features. "I need you to talk to Will."

He hadn't been expecting that. "About what?"

She dropped into a kitchen chair and held a thick white mug of coffee cupped between her palms.

"About how he has to keep a low profile until the police and the FBI say he can come out of the shadows and get back to his life. About how he can't go off roaming into Royal like he tried to do just an hour ago."

Jesse's eyes went wide, and he shot a hard look at the main house behind him before looking back to his mother. "He can't go into town. What's he thinking? We already told him he's got to stay here on the ranch until things are figured out."

"Yes, I know." Her eyebrows arched. "I was there."

Sighing, he nodded. "Yes ma'am."

But Cora Lee wasn't finished. "Will's going stir-crazy I think. All he can talk about is getting out there and hunting down Richard Lowell himself. Will wants to reclaim his life."

Still furious, Jesse thought about Rich, a man who had duped them all. It was Will himself who'd figured out who the impostor was. When he heard that the man had claimed Rich had died in the boating accident, he'd known it was Rich himself who had stolen his life. Who but Will and Rich would have known the details? Now they were all trapped in this helplessness.

Jesse couldn't blame his younger brother for wanting to do something. Anything. He could understand the frustration and the fury. Hell, he shared it. Richard Lowell. Hard to believe that he was the man who'd impersonated Will for so long.

Rich and Will had met at college and become friends, but apparently that hadn't been enough for Rich. The man had been so eaten up by envy or whatever the hell it was that psychos got eaten up by, that eventually, he'd tried to kill Will and take over his life. And he'd come damn close to pulling it off forever.

"I know how Will feels," Jesse muttered. "I'd like to find that bastard—excuse me—too and let him know what a world of hurt really feels like."

"You think I don't?" Cora Lee's features were frozen into a mask of ice and steel. "Richard Lowell almost killed one of my sons. Stole from us. Used us. If I had him here in front of me right now, I can't say that I wouldn't reach back into time for a little frontier justice."

Jesse smiled grimly as he nodded in agreement. "But we can't. Will can't. Not yet anyway and he's just going to have to suck it up. Hell, for all we know, Rich is in that damn urn."

But even as he said it, Jesse hoped that wasn't true. He really wanted to make Rich Lowell pay for hurting his family.

"Agreed," Cora Lee snapped, taking a sip of her black coffee. "And it's pretty much what I told him an hour ago. Would have had better luck talking to a boulder. Maybe it'd help if *you* tell him."

"I can do that." Jesse left his mother's cottage and started for the main house. Moonlight lit his way, but he didn't need it. He could have found his way over any part of this ranch blindfolded. Jesse knew every stone, every tree, every damn speck of dirt on this land as well as he knew his own bedroom. It was his home. His life.

Already wired way too tight, Jesse felt like he was walking a fine line of control. Which meant he was in the perfect mood for a confrontation with his little brother.

Jillian glanced at baby Mac and smiled. The little girl had her very own paintbrush and was applying fresh green paint to the wall—though she was getting more on herself. What her daughter lacked in talent she made up for in enthusiasm.

Silly to start painting tonight and Jillian knew it. But she hadn't been able to stand it.

"Just one wall," she told herself. She'd do the rest of the work tomorrow, but for tonight, she really wanted to see how the color would look on the boring beige walls.

Already, the apartment was taking on a different look. Of course that had a lot to do with the things Jillian had found while out shopping with Lucy. Not that she was spending tons of money—she'd found a few great items at the consignment shop and then had splurged at a discount store and bought a few pots and pans and a four-piece set of dishes, along with a new crib for Mac. Everything else they needed, Jillian figured she would buy a little at a time.

"The important thing here is," she said to Mac, "I have a job, we have a home and some wonderful new friends. Isn't that right, baby girl?"

Mac whipped her head around to look at her mother. A stray splash of green paint swiped across her little cheek and her green eyes danced with joy. "Jesse? And horsies?"

Jillian swallowed hard and told herself to distract her daughter. "And your friend Brody, remember?"

"Jesse!" Mac crowed the word and dragged her paintbrush against the wall again.

It looked like Jillian wasn't the only one in the family who was a little obsessed with Jesse Navarro. Now, she told herself, she had *two* hearts to protect.

Sighing, she set her brush down, walked to her daughter and swept the girl up into her arms. Staring into that beautiful little face, Jillian said, "Let's get you ready for sleep in your new bed, okay?"

Mac tipped her head to one side, her wispy blond hair waving with the movement. Touching her mother's cheek with her little hand, she smiled. "Jesse?"

"No, no Jesse tonight," Jillian answered and felt horrible when Mac's tiny mouth moved into a pout with a quivering bottom lip.

"Want Jesse." Mac's head dropped to her mother's shoulder in disappointment.

"Me, too, baby," Jillian whispered. "That's the problem."

* * *

Inside the main house, Jesse stalked across the entryway into the great room and stopped on the threshold, taking a long look at the familiar room.

Cora Lee had decorated this room as a family gathering place, so she'd made sure it was comfortable, welcoming and able to withstand dirty cowboy boots.

The overstuffed furniture, covered in dark red, deep blue and forest green fabrics, boasted deep, soft cushions. Hand-carved oak tables held books, magazines and a few of Brody's toys. Brass lamps with Tiffany glass shades threw puddles of golden light on the floor and the shadow of color on the walls. A man-height stone fireplace took up one wall and on the opposite side of the room a gigantic flat-screen TV took up most of the wall space. There were couches and chairs scattered all around the room, just waiting for a crowd to drop by and settle in.

Framed family photos dotted the tables and the walls, and colorful, braided rugs spread across the wood floor. There were bookshelves ringing the wide room and two cushioned window seats that during the day provided a wide view of the ranch yard. Tucked into one corner of the room was a bar where crystal decanters filled with whiskey, brandy and vodka glinted in the light. The hearth was empty and cold—about how his insides felt.

Will was slumped in a chair set close to the fireplace, a crystal tumbler of whiskey in one hand. Here in this room, the lamplight and the fire kept the darkness outside the windows at bay. The wind kicked up suddenly, wailing as it passed beneath the eaves, and Jesse made a mental note to have one of his men check the shingles on the barn roof tomorrow. When the wind was strong enough, sometimes he swore it could carry off the horses.

But for right now, he had a brother to confront. Will wore jeans, a blue T-shirt and his favorite brown boots—currently propped up on the coffee table in front of him. He looked at home. Where he belonged. Fake Will had moved off the ranch to Megan's house after their marriage and Jesse hadn't been able to figure that one out, blaming it on Will's grief and taking time to recover from the accident. Now, of course, it made sense.

Will lifted his glass, took a drink, then silently saluted Jesse's entrance.

"Welcome to my gilded cage," he said.

Jesse scowled at him and crossed the room, his steps muffled by the rugs strewn across the floor. "What the hell is wrong with you?"

Will studied the amber liquid in the glass as if searching for an answer to that question. Then he gave it up and shrugged. "Hell, what could be wrong? I'm alive. Back home. Married to a woman I hardly know. *Trapped*."

"Trapped." Jesse walked closer, slapped Will's

feet off the table and sat there himself, staring at his brother. "How are you trapped?"

"Are you kidding?" He took another drink and shook his head. "I can't even go into Royal for lunch at the diner. I'm stuck here on the ranch while that bastard Rich Lowell is off living God knows where. What about that seems right to you?"

"None of it. But you know why it's like this. Enough people already know what's going on," Jesse said, voice hard and tight. "Everyone who was at your funeral knows you're actually alive. We've got a lid on them, but you go strolling through Royal, the rest of the town finds out. With all the gossips around here, not to mention the media that loves to get the dirt on the top families in Royal—somehow word would reach Lowell before the cops can find him. Then he'd disappear and we'd never get his ass back to Texas."

"Right, so the thief who tried to kill me is free to go where he wants and I'm serving jail time." Will snorted and shook his head, taking another sip of his scotch. "He pushes me off my own damn boat in the middle of a storm and leaves me for dead. I'm in a damn coma in Mexico for months while he's here—"

He broke off, dragged in a breath and pushed one hand through his hair. "While he's *here* living *my* life and nobody—" he fixed a hard glare on Jesse "—not even my damn *family* notices that he's an *impostor*?"

That last bit Jesse knew he had coming. Hell,

sometimes he couldn't believe himself that he hadn't known the impostor wasn't his brother. But Rich had done a damn good job of pretending to be Will. The man had not only fooled the Sanders, but the whole damn town of Royal.

"Yeah, well, I wasn't expecting a fake brother, was I?" he asked in his own defense. Pitiful and he knew it, but it was all he had. "Rich clearly had had surgery and he even explained away why his voice didn't sound like yours. He had excuses for everything, damn it." Jesse grabbed Will's scotch and took a long drink. "He even fooled Mom and that's not easy."

"Doesn't make me feel any better," Will muttered, grabbing his drink back. "When I finally woke up from that damn coma, I didn't know who I was. It took me forever to remember, all the while learning how to walk and move again and when I finally get home to my loving family, I find them burying me."

That had been a weird day for the ages.

"Glad we didn't. Bury you, that is."

"Who the hell is in that urn?" Will demanded.

That question had been bugging Jesse for the last couple of weeks at least and he was no closer to getting an answer than he had been the day Will had walked into the funeral. "Could be Rich."

"I wish," Will muttered. "I think."

"Could be *anybody*," Jesse continued. "With what he did to you, Lowell proved he's not afraid to murder someone. Could be one of his victims or a damn homeless man he thought no one would miss."

"None of this seems real."

"I know what you mean," Jesse said. "You know they sent the urn to the FBI for DNA testing."

"How're they going to test *ashes*?" Will demanded.

"Hell if I know," Jesse admitted. "But apparently there's usually enough bone and teeth left that we might get lucky. Get an identification."

Will sighed and took another sip of his drink. "Don't know if I hope it's Rich or not. Dead, I couldn't beat him with my fists. Which is something I really want to do."

"Get in line." Jesse grabbed the glass again and took another drink.

"Get your own," Will snarled and snatched the glass back. "You know, it won't be him in that urn. He's too slick to die. He's out there. *Somewhere.*" He stared into his drink again, then lifted his gaze to Jesse. "Not only did Rich steal from me and damn near kill me, but he screwed with my name. My reputation. Married Megan. He made me look like an ass."

Will looked tired, but more than that, he looked as though he'd been hanging on to a cliff's edge for too long and his grip was slipping. Jesse could sympathize. But he couldn't let his brother wallow, either. It was hard to accept any of this, but the sooner Will did, the sooner they could all get through this and back to normal. "What Rich did wasn't your fault."

"Feels like it is," Will muttered. "It was *my* name he was throwing around. He got Jillian pregnant pretending to be me, then walked out on her, leaving her to try emailing me for help—the *real* me, before the boating accident—" Will stopped and scrubbed one hand across his face. "Which is pretty much when Rich decided I was in his way. He hit me over the head and tossed me into the ocean right after I got Jillian's email. He must have known I'd figure it all out."

Jesse felt for his brother. He knew what it was to have pride in your name. Your honor. Their father had taught them that if a man couldn't be trusted, he wasn't a man at all. But Will hadn't actually done any of this. "And you were supposed to stop that how?"

"I don't know." Will shot him a hard look. "Stop using logic when I feel crappy."

Jesse nodded sagely. "Feeling sorry for yourself, you mean."

"Who has more right?" Will countered and jumped to his feet. Handing the scotch off to Jesse, he started pacing, shaking his head, muttering. "A man I thought was a friend stole my damn life."

Jesse finished off his brother's scotch in one deep swallow and relished the burn of the liquor on its way down. Setting the empty glass aside, he stared at Will and tried to get his own anger under control.

Wouldn't do a damn bit of good for both of them to be furious and powerless to do anything about it.

But nothing stirred Jesse's temper like someone messing with his family.

"Yeah, he did," Jesse agreed. "But that's done now."

"Is it?" Will spun around to glare at him. "Hell, the ramifications keep tumbling down on me like somebody knocked over a domino and a whole long line of 'em are tipping over in succession—and they're all landing on my head."

"I know."

"I've even got a damn wife!" Will shouted, tossing both hands high. "I don't even know Megan Phillips Sanders, but we're married—"

"In name only," Jesse pointed out, knowing it didn't mean a thing because Will and Megan had to stay married—at least for the time being. They couldn't risk gossip no matter what it cost Will. He wished to hell he could do something to fix it.

"What difference does it make?" Will shoved both hands into his jeans pockets and let his head fall back until he was staring up at the beamed ceiling. "Rich married her using my name, so it's still a legal marriage to a woman I don't know."

"The lawyers are working on it."

"Well, that's comforting," he snarled. "And in the meantime, what the hell do I say to her?"

"Why don't you let her do the talking? Shut up

long enough for her to tell you what happened." Jesse rattled the single ice cube in the glass. Standing up, he stared at his younger brother. "Making yourself nuts isn't going to solve a damn thing. You know that, right? So listen to what Megan has to say."

"Yeah, yeah, I can do that." Nodding, Will still looked furious as he suddenly snapped. "So, did you stand up for me at my wedding?"

"What?"

"I'm asking if you were best man to a stranger pretending to be me?" His eyes glinted with banked fury.

"No. You—*they* got married in Reno. The family wasn't invited."

Eyes wide, jaw dropped, Will asked, "And you didn't think that was weird?"

"Yeah, I did." Jesse met temper with temper. Damned if he'd take any more guilt heaped on him. Rich had fooled everyone. Did he like admitting that he'd been had? No. But the truth was, he hadn't been the only one fooled. "Hell, you'd been acting weird for a long time, so I wasn't surprised. Mom was hurt, but she wasn't shocked at the lack of an invitation, either. You cut the family out of your life, Will. You were never here. Flying all over the damn world, never showing up for work, drinking too much when you were here—"

"Yeah," Will interrupted, eyes flashing, "but that wasn't *me*."

"Well, we didn't know that, did we?" Jesse countered, glancing into the empty glass on the table, wishing it was full. "Rich was smart enough to make himself scarce. He didn't spend much time in Texas and almost no time at all at the ranch..."

Will pushed both hands through his hair. "This is like a nightmare I can't wake up from."

"What the hell do you want me to say?" The final threads of Jesse's patience unraveled. "Rich screwed all of us over. We'll get past it. I'm glad as hell you're back. Sorry if everything's not great, but you're alive. And thinking you were dead nearly killed Mom."

Will scowled as it looked like all the air left him.

Jesse took a breath and sighed. Voice softer, temper controlled, he said, "The whole family went through hell until you walked into your own damn funeral. If you expect me to feel sorry for you that you're alive and have a mess to fix, then you got a long wait coming."

Will's gaze met Jesse's. "Fine, but—"

"No." Jesse braced his feet wide apart and crossed his arms over his chest. He stared at his younger brother until Will shifted uncomfortably under his steady gaze. "You had your say and you've had time to pull it together."

"Yeah?" Will snorted.

"None of this is gonna be straightened out overnight."

"It's been two and a half weeks," he reminded Jesse.

"You were gone nearly two years. Might take more than a few weeks to fix things." Jesse narrowed his gaze on his brother. "So stop whining."

Insulted, Will blurted, "I don't whine."

"Could've fooled me," Jesse said tightly. He knew his brother and sympathy wasn't what he needed. "You don't like being stuck on the ranch. I get it."

"Wow." Will nodded. "Thanks."

He ignored the sarcasm. "But you don't have a choice. You've got to keep a low profile. Don't let anyone beyond those who were at the funeral and saw you already know you're alive. Until we know if Rich is still alive and still pretending to be you—or if he's the one in that damn urn…the cops are on it and they'll find the bastard eventually."

"Eventually," Will repeated under his breath. "How long? A year? Two? *Ten?*"

Shaking his head, Jesse said, "Get over yourself. It's not going to be that long."

"Yeah. Hopefully not. It's just that I feel so damn helpless," Will admitted, his voice a low rumble. "That's the hardest part to swallow."

"I hear that," Jesse said. "Felt the same way myself when I thought you were dead. Felt it again when you came home and we realized we'd been taken in by a thief and liar. Feel it now when I'm trying to talk my little brother off a damn ledge."

A second or two passed before Will nodded. "I'm not on a ledge. I'm…okay, I'm *whining.* Fine. I get the message." He frowned then. "And what's this 'little' brother stuff? You're one inch taller than me."

"Don't you forget it," Jesse said with a grin. "Just like I'm the oldest."

"Yeah." Will nodded sagely and tipped his head to one side, pretending to study Jesse carefully. "You've got five years on me, and brother, it's starting to show."

"What?"

"Yeah. You're getting old."

He knew Will was riding him and it felt good to have this dynamic back again. Damned if he hadn't missed ragging on his younger brother and having the insults tossed back at him. "I'm thirty-five, not sixty-five."

Will shrugged. "You know what they say, once you pass thirty, it's all downhill."

"Then hang on," Jesse told him, "your turn for the downhill slide starts this year."

"Some of us handle it better."

"Like you've been 'handling' everything else lately?" Jesse asked.

Will sighed. "Damn, you're like a dog with a bone. I already said you're right. I was wrong. I'll shut up and play along. I won't be happy about it, but I'll do it. I'll stop worrying Mom. I'll suck it up and be a good prisoner until we find Rich Lowell.

Then," he said, features tightening, eyes narrowing, "I'm gonna beat that bastard so hard..."

"I'll help you," Jesse said.

"I know you will," his brother said. Will took a deep breath and said, "So. Change of subject. Even I can only talk about me for so long. I saw Jillian Norris was here again today."

"Yeah." Jesse turned for the wet bar against the far wall. Now that the storm was over, he could use his own drink.

"She get settled into the apartment all right?"

"Yeah, I took her and the little girl over there yesterday—" He poured two fingers of scotch then walked back to refill Will's glass, as well. "Speaking of those apartments, we've gotta do something there. Depressing as hell. I mean, small is one thing, but I swear it looks like every jail cell in every movie I've ever seen."

"That bad?"

"I thought so." Jesse took a drink. "I offered to get her something else, but she refused. Said it would do fine for her and Mac."

"Then it will."

Jesse snorted and took another drink. "You didn't see it."

"I'll take your word for it. We can hire someone to fix it. Hell, if it's that bad, we'll get all of the apartments in that building updated." Will walked across the room, refilled his own glass and then asked, "Back to Jillian though… Had a busy day. Interview at the TCC, new apartment, then back here to watch you give her daughter a riding lesson."

Jesse studied the scotch as he tipped the glass from side to side, making tiny, amber waves that sloshed against the crystal. "Lucy got her a job interview at the TCC day care."

"Uh-huh."

"And I promised Mac she could ride a horse."

"Uh-huh."

"Then Lucy and Jillian went shopping and left Mac here with Mom."

"Uh-huh."

Irritated now, Jesse snapped, "Is there something you want to say?"

Outside, the wind howled while Will affected an innocent pose that Jesse wasn't buying for an instant.

"No," his brother said, taking a sip of his scotch. "I just have plenty of extra time to study things now."

"Is that right? And just what are you studying?"

Will shrugged. "Not studying so much as noticing. Like the fact that Jillian Norris is really hot."

Jesse scowled at him. Like he needed Will to tell him about Jillian. Hadn't Jesse's dreams been full of her for the last few weeks? Didn't he wake up every damn morning with his body hard as stone and his blood steaming just under his skin? And just why the hell was Will "noticing" her anyway?

"That woman's legs must be a mile long," Will

mused. "And that's just in her jeans. Can't help wondering what she'd look like in a dress..."

To hell with a dress. Jesse wanted to know what she looked like naked. Stretched across his bed, wrapping those long legs around his hips and pulling him deep inside her.

"Then there's her *hair*," Will said. "Always caught up in that ponytail. Makes you want to see how long it is when it's loose and hanging down her back..."

Or fisted in his hands, Jesse added silently. "Is there a point to this?" His hand tightened on the tumbler he held.

"No point." A half smile curved Will's mouth. "Just a couple of observations. But you know, maybe I should give her a call. Make sure she's happy with that apartment. If it's as bad as you say it is..."

Jesse stiffened. If anyone was going to be checking up on Jillian, it was going to be *him*. "Yeah, I'll take care of it. If you're so anxious to call a woman, call your *wife*. Let me worry about Jillian."

"Uh-huh." Will smothered a grin, but not fast enough to keep Jesse from noticing it.

"What's so damn funny?"

"Not a thing." His brother held up one hand in peace. "I'm just saying, she's a gorgeous woman is all."

"Am I blind suddenly?" Jesse demanded. "I can't see a beautiful woman so you and Mom have to point it out to me?"

"Mom, too, huh?" Will nodded. "Interesting."

Irritated with himself and his whole family, Jesse snapped, "No, it's not interesting. There's *nothing* interesting, damn it."

"Yeah, I'm convinced." Grinning now, Will walked back to his chair, sat down and propped his boots up on the coffee table again. Turning his gaze to Jesse, he said, "Beautiful woman, great kid who already likes you, yeah, nothing to see here."

Jesse's gaze shot to his brother's. Now he saw the same speculative gleam in Will's eyes that he'd seen on his mother's face just a little while ago.

Well, they could just get over it. He wasn't looking at Jillian any more than any other red-blooded male would. He could appreciate a hot woman with great legs, a wide mouth, full breasts and a first-class behind without it meaning anything. His insides fisted, and his groin went hard enough that his jeans felt like torture.

Fine. He wanted her. He could admit that—to himself. But want didn't mean anything. It was temporary. Want could be eased by having. And that was what this was coming to. But being with Jillian wasn't going to turn out like his mother and brother were clearly hoping. He wasn't looking for a family.

Jesse already had Brody to look out for. He owed that boy because if it hadn't been for Jesse, Brody's daddy wouldn't have died. So his job now was to be there for Lucy. For her son. He didn't have the right to go looking for something just for himself. Selfish needs had to be buried for the sake of doing the right thing.

But knowing that didn't make this any easier. Tossing the rest of his scotch down his throat, he set the glass down and headed for the door.

"Where're you going?" Will called after him.

"Home." *To take a cold shower.*

Five

The first day at Jillian's new job went great.

She loved working with Ginger and the two other women, Patti and Teresa. The kids were terrific, with only a couple of tantrums thrown here and there, and best of all, Mac was with her during the day and making friends already. Jillian had a good feeling about how this was going.

When she'd first come to Royal she'd hoped only for a settlement from her baby's father. Instead, she'd found friends who had helped her get started on a whole new life—and she was eager to make the most of it. Already, her apartment felt like home as she and Mac decorated and made it their own. Not long ago, she'd worried about the future, and now, all she saw were possibilities.

She even enjoyed her new routine. People could complain and say their daily chores were a rut, but to Jillian, a rut just meant "comfort zone." Every morning on the way to work, she stopped at the Royal diner to get herself a cup of coffee and some chocolate milk for Mac. And what really pleased Jillian was that already she was being treated like a regular. Now she and her baby girl were part of other people's routines.

Only that morning, Amanda Battle had called out a hello and said she had Jillian's order ready to go. It was a special kind of feeling, Jillian told herself, knowing that she was finally in a place where she and Mac could belong. Far from the neon and crowds of Vegas, in this small town, she could build something good and strong for her and her daughter.

Letting her gaze sweep around the bright room filled with young voices, she felt more confident about her life than she ever had before.

With one exception.

Her mind kept drifting to thoughts of Jesse Navarro.

She'd tried to stop, but her brain was working against her. And not just her brain. Her own body was traitorous, too. Every night, when she tried to sleep, her subconscious provided image after image of Jesse. His thick dark hair. Chocolate eyes. That cowboy hat pulled low on his forehead. The way faded jeans clung to muscular, long legs…

"Miss Jill!" Small hands tugging at her black slacks, an excitable voice calling a shortened version of her name since the tiny ones had too much trouble with *Jillian.* A little boy jumping up and down, looking at her with desperation in his eyes and just like that, her fantasies were dead, supplanted by reality.

"What is it, Cole?" she asked, crouching so she could look the three-year-old in the eye.

"Potty!" He danced in place as if to let her know he really meant it.

"Oh!" No time to waste. Jillian straightened quickly and started moving. Taking him by the hand, she said, "Okay, let's go," and headed for the bathroom. Then the front door opened, and she stopped dead as Jesse Navarro walked into the room.

A moment ago, she'd been thinking about him and now here he was. The universe was toying with her. Nerves hurtled through her stomach in a blink and her grasp tightened slightly on Cole's hand. "Jesse. What are you doing here?"

"Making a delivery," he said and stepped aside. Brody raced in, grinning. "Hi, Miss Jill! Surprise!"

"Hi, Brody, it's so nice to see you." She looked up at Jesse again as concern whipped through her suddenly. "We weren't expecting Brody today. Is Lucy all right?"

"She's fine. Got a meeting with an architect is

all and can't really get the work done with—" he paused to give Brody a knowing look "—this little distraction running around. Mom's off to Dallas for the day, so…"

"I get to play," Brody explained and took off for the far corner where the train set was stored.

"Miss Jill…" Cole's voice, even more urgent.

Right. She'd forgotten. To Jesse, she said, "I'll, uh, be right back."

A slight smile curved his mouth. "You go ahead. I'll wait."

Heart racing, stomach spinning, Jillian hurried Cole to the bathroom. By the time she returned, Jesse was perched uneasily on one of the kid-sized chairs sprinkled around the room. Mac sat on his lap, excitedly telling him a story. Her little hands waved, her eyes sparkled, and Jesse was giving her his complete attention.

Not fair, she thought. Not fair that a man that gorgeous, that dangerous, could be such a softie with her daughter. Most men she'd known put on a show of paying attention to Mac, just to get in good with Jillian. But it didn't take long before their eyes slid away, their patience dissolved, and soon, it was clear that they either didn't like children or simply didn't want to be bothered with them.

Jesse was different.

Damn it.

Not only did he affect Jillian on an almost cellular level, but he *cared* about Mac. Yes, he was good with Brody, too, but the little boy was his nephew. She would expect him to be kind and patient with family. The fact that he showed the same attention to her little girl really touched Jillian's heart. And that was dangerous.

As if he sensed her watching him, Jesse slowly turned his head and met her gaze. Even from across the room crowded with noisy children, Jillian felt the quick jolt of heat that raced from the center of her chest right down to the soles of her feet. A fire burned in her belly and just below, she felt the ache of need pulse into life.

Oh, don't do this, Jillian. She had a job, an apartment and the start of a brand-new life. *That's what you need to focus on. Not the gorgeous cowboy that makes you burn.* Her internal voice was stern, and she fervently hoped that this time, she'd listen to that voice rather than ignoring it.

"Horsies?"

Jillian heard her little girl and sighed. Mac had a serious crush on horses—and the cowboy who'd introduced her to them.

"When you come back to the ranch, you can ride the horse again, all right?"

Satisfied with that, Mac squirmed off Jesse's lap then ran to the corner to play with Brody. Not only was her daughter getting too attached to Jesse, but she was clearly starting to think of Brody as a big brother.

She turned back in time to see Jesse lever himself out of the child-sized chair. He headed right for her, and she could only think that watching him move was like seeing a lion slowly uncoil himself and get ready to— Okay, maybe not attack, but to stalk. Not that Jesse was a stalker or anything, it was just— Oh *stop*, Jillian.

When he was close enough, she took a breath and told herself to get a grip. She wasn't some timid virgin, for heaven's sake. But even as she reassured herself, she had to admit that she'd never dealt with a man who was so completely *male*.

"What's the matter?" Jesse watched her, a quizzical expression on his face.

"What? Nothing. Really." Jillian shook her head, took a breath and told her racing heart to slow the hell down.

"Okay." He didn't look as though he believed her, but he let it go. "Lucy will be here in a couple of hours to pick up Brody."

"Sure. That's fine." He was standing so close to her that she could see tiny gold flecks in his dark chocolate eyes. Why hadn't she noticed them before?

"Got a lot of kids in here today."

Safe subject. Good.

Jillian let her gaze sweep over the children in the

big, bright room. "I know. Apparently there's some big dance here at the TCC in a couple days."

He nodded. "The black-tie gala."

She turned and glanced at him. "That's it. Well, some moms are out shopping for it and others are working here, getting ready for the big event." She shrugged and smiled. "So, we've got a full house. I don't mind, though. I love kids."

"It shows."

Jillian tipped her head to one side, looking at him.

He shrugged. "Most people would be dangling by the thread of their last nerve surrounded by this many hyper kids."

"They're not hyper," she corrected. "They're just excited to be with so many friends."

"Whichever," he said, shaking his head. "Seems like hard work to me."

"Harder than training wild horses?"

He laughed unexpectedly, and the deep sound of it rolled over her, lighting up every cell in her body. What a smile did for that handsome face of his should be illegal. Or at least come with a warning label.

"Oh, yeah. Give me a mean horse any day over this many kids all at once."

"You're terrific with Brody and Mac," she reminded him.

His smile slowly faded as he turned to look at those two children in the crowd. "They're different."

Before she could ask him what he meant, he set his hat on his head and said, "I've got to go. Things to do at the ranch."

"Okay…" She watched him turn for the door and wondered what had made him change so abruptly from teasing laughter to shadows in his eyes and a curtain dropping over his features.

"Jesse?"

He stopped and looked over his shoulder at her.

With his gaze on hers, Jillian couldn't think of anything to say. And since she felt like an idiot, she finally said, "Nothing. Goodbye."

"Yeah. Bye." He left then, and Jillian couldn't look away as he walked to his truck, climbed in and drove off.

Probably wasn't a good sign that her heart was still racing.

By the time Lucy came to pick up Brody, Jillian had had a long day. As much as she loved her darling daughter and every other child in the day care, she wanted half an hour of silence all to herself. It was all Jesse's fault, she told herself. She'd been doing fine until he showed up with his black cowboy hat, scuffed boots and whiskery jaws. After that, she'd had to work twice as hard to concentrate on the kids who needed her, because her mind kept dragging her back to Jesse.

"You look a little ragged," Lucy said, hugging her son to her side while she talked.

"It's been a day," Jillian admitted, though she didn't tell Lucy that it was Jesse making her a little crazed. "The kids are great, don't get me wrong, but—"

"A break would be nice?" Lucy asked.

"Heaven," Jillian agreed, glancing around the room. Most of the kids had been picked up already. There were only four left now waiting for their parents. The noise level in the room had dropped dramatically, but still, Jillian longed for quiet.

"I can fix that," Lucy said.

"What?"

"I'll take Mac with me. I've got an extra car seat in the truck—" She grinned. "Sometimes Brody's friends need a ride. Like today for example."

Jillian shook her head, automatically refusing the generous offer. She just wasn't used to this level of friendship and though she liked it, it was going to take some getting accustomed to. "You don't have to do that."

Lucy smiled. "I know. But I just had three solid hours of a break. The least I can do is return the favor."

Jillian laughed. "You weren't on a break. Jesse told me you had a meeting."

"Yes, but I was talking horses! Trust me, that's a break."

Not surprising that the whole Sanders family seemed crazy about horses. They did live on one of the biggest ranches in Texas.

"Did you get your breeding/rescue barn all figured out?" Jillian knew absolutely nothing about horses or how to care for them, but she was interested in her friend.

"We did," Lucy said eagerly. "It's going to be gorgeous." She paused. "Bigger than I'd expected it to be, but that's okay. Just means I can rescue more horses."

"That's what's really motivating you, isn't it?" Jillian asked. "I noticed the other day when you were talking about this that you seemed more excited by the prospect of saving animals than you were by the breeding program."

"I'm that obvious, am I?" Lucy laughed a little. "I guess I am. It's so…satisfying—and that's not the right word, either—to help neglected animals get healthy and happy again. I just—"

"You don't have to explain."

"Good, because I don't think I can." Shaking her head, Lucy hugged Brody, still attached to her left leg. Looking down at him, she said, "Brody honey, why don't you go get Mac and we'll head home."

"Oh, Lucy—"

"No argument. We can have a drink when you come to pick her up later."

"That does sound good," Jillian said, sighing.

“Excellent. Hi, sweetie!” Mac and Brody raced up together, Brody in the lead and dragging the little girl behind him. “Do you want to go to the ranch for a little while?”

“Jesse!” Mac looked up at Jillian and grinned. “Horsies!”

Jillian sighed again. It seemed that despite knowing she should keep her distance from Jesse, she was destined to be thrown into his path.

“Sounds like someone’s got a crush,” Lucy mused, her gaze fixed on Jillian, not Mac.

“He’s so good with her…”

“Handsome, too.”

“Yeah, he really is—” Jillian broke off and glared at her friend.

Lucy was unashamed. “Hey, just wanted to see if there was anyone else with a crush and now I’m thinking there might be.”

“Crush!” Mac yelled, and Jillian winced.

“I really like you, Lucy, but you’re wrong.”

“Sure I am. I can see that now.”

“You’re incorrigible.”

“Isn’t it great?” Lucy grinned, leaned down and scooped Mac up into her arms. “I don’t plan to change, either. When I’m old and gray I’ll be nosy, opinionated and people will run when they see me coming.”

Jillian had to laugh. “I believe you.”

"Mom, I want ice cream," Brody said, tugging on the hem of her black shirt.

"What a great idea! Mac, you want some ice cream, too?"

"Cream!"

"I think that's a yes," Jillian said, giving her daughter a smile.

"This is why I hang out with kids. They know what's good," Lucy mused. "We'll see you later, Jillian."

"I'll come to the ranch as soon as I'm off work and—"

"*That* is not a break," Lucy chided, shaking her head. "Take some time. Relax. Do nothing for a while. You are not allowed to show up at the ranch before at least seven."

Laughing, Jillian admitted, "I don't know if I remember *how* to do nothing."

"Give it a shot." She headed for the door, both kids in tow. "Say bye."

"Bye, Mama, bye!" Mac waved frantically, and Brody did the same. And when they were gone, Jillian felt a pang that was a mixture of relief and trepidation.

To pick up her little girl, she'd have to see Jesse again, and that was getting harder and harder. Because every time she saw him, her mind dredged up images that she had no business entertaining. She imagined his body covering hers, his big, callused hands sliding across her skin. His mouth on hers, tongues tangling in a wild, desperate dance. Her blood burned, her heartbeat quickened and her mouth went dry.

"Jillian?"

She jolted, dragging her completely aroused self out of her daydream and turned to face Ginger.

"You okay?" the older woman asked.

"Probably not," Jillian murmured.

"What?"

"Nothing, nothing." Taking a deep breath, she emptied her mind and hurried over to keep three-year-old Colton Jackson from eating a crayon.

Jesse and his ranch foreman, Carlos, were in a dead heat. Horses neck and neck as they raced back to the ranch after checking on the herd in the south pasture. The end-of-the-ride race was tradition, with pride and bragging rights the only rewards. Days like this reminded Jesse how lucky he was to live the life he loved. The ranch. The wide-open stretches of land. The horses. Being outside as another storm rolled in with electricity alive in the air. The thunder of the horses' hooves against the earth sounded like drum beats. The wind in his face smelled of the coming rain. Sunset stained the sky red and purple and gold. And he loved it all.

He heard the cowboys cheer as they passed and Jesse grinned. He had this one. His horse was younger, stronger than Carlos's mount—and Jesse liked to win. Hell, he'd lost only one of these races in the last two months.

"Go boss, you got him."

"Come on, Carlos," someone else called, "don't let him win again!"

Laughing, feeling the rush of a fast horse and the wind in his face, Jesse beat Carlos into the ranch yard by a nose and pulled back on the reins to ease his horse into slowing down.

"You got me," Carlos said, laughing. "But tomorrow I take the stallion and you ride this lazy gelding."

"It's not the horse, Carlos." Jesse held out one hand. "It's the rider."

Still laughing, Carlos shook then warned, "Tomorrow it'll be different."

"Keep hope alive." Jesse swung down from his horse, handed the reins over to Carlos who would get the horses cooled down and stabled. Being out with the men, focusing on the work of keeping such a big ranch running well cleared his mind, gave him peace—however briefly. It wiped away worries about Will, guilt over Lucy and Brody and even numbed the thoughts of Jillian that were now almost constant. Now that he was back, work over for the day, he knew she would crowd his mind again and there was no way to stop it. No way to pretend he didn't enjoy it.

Scowling a little, he told Carlos, "I'll be by later to check on Dancer."

The mare was close to delivering her foal, and Jesse wanted to make sure everything was as it should be. He knew the local vet, Scarlett McKittrick, could be here in fifteen minutes if he needed her help, but chances were good Dancer would manage the labor and birth on her own as horses had been doing for millennia.

"I think it'll be much later, boss." Carlos looked past Jesse and nodded, a faint smile on his face. "Looks like you've got some company."

Jesse turned and felt a hard punch slam into his chest. A hell of a lot of good it did him trying to put her out of his mind when she could show up out of nowhere and knock him off his feet. Jillian stood there beside that beat-up Honda of hers, holding what looked to be a foil-covered plate. Not that he cared what she was holding. He just liked looking at her.

Jesse had seen Mac with Brody earlier and had known that sooner or later, the little girl's mother would be arriving to get her. And right now, he was glad as hell he'd come in from the pasture when he had. Otherwise he might have missed her.

When that thought settled in, Jesse frowned to himself. He didn't like that he cared whether or not he saw the woman, but the feeling was there whether he wanted to admit it or not. But now wasn't the time to worry about that. Instead, he filled his gaze with the woman who was driving him nuts lately.

Her long blond hair was in the ever-present ponytail that was beginning to really get to him. Nothing he wanted more than to free all that hair and run his fingers through it, watch it frame her face. He wanted to know how long it was, and how it looked lying against her bare skin.

She wore a dark red shirt, blue jeans, and stylish boots. With the hard wind blowing, the ends of her hair lifted and twisted as if dancing.

As he walked toward her, he watched her wide mouth curve into a smile that set a fire in the pit of his belly. It took everything he had to keep from giving in to the urge to grab hold of her and finally taste that mouth.

"You won." She shook a few windblown tendrils of hair out of her face and looked up into his eyes.

"Yeah." He grinned and tossed a look over his shoulder to where Carlos was leading the horses toward the barn. "This time anyway. You here to pick up Mac?"

"Yes," she said, "but I wanted to see you first."

Interesting. "Why's that?"

"I wanted to thank you," she said, holding out the foil-covered plate. "You've been so good to Mac, letting her ride the horses she loves. Helping me find that apartment—"

"Don't thank me for *that*." He shook his head.

"Still can't believe you wanted to stay in that grim little place."

She laughed. "The apartment's fine and I appreciate it."

Frowning a little, he said, "Either way, you don't have to thank me."

"I already have." She was still holding the plate out, so Jesse took it.

"Heavy."

"Glass pie plate," she said.

"Pie?" Both eyebrows winged up. "You bought me a pie?"

"I didn't buy it," she told him, slightly insulted. "I made it. And I want that pie plate back when you're finished."

"Really?" He couldn't remember the last time a woman had given him anything, let alone something she'd taken the time and trouble to make herself. Pleasure shone in her eyes, and Jesse thought she just kept getting more beautiful. Then, pushing that stray thought aside, he lifted the edge of the foil and briefly looked at the golden crust before carefully covering the pie again. "What kind is it?"

She took a deep breath, tucked her hands into her pockets and said, "It's my specialty. Spiced cherry."

He looked into her eyes. "You have a specialty?"

"I do and you'll love it."

"Sounds good."

She met his gaze. "It's better than good."

Looking into those smoky green eyes of hers, Jesse felt another twist of heat down low in his gut. It wasn't pie he was thinking of now. He had a feeling that if he ever got his hands on her *she* would be better than good, too.

"Come on. We'll go to my place and I can taste this pie.," When she glanced toward the main house as if deciding whether or not she should go and get Mac right away, he added, "Mac's playing with Brody. You can take a few minutes. See if I like this pie. I happen to be a pie-eating expert. I can tell you if it's any good or not."

"I'm not worried," she said proudly, lifting her chin slightly. "That's the best pie you've ever eaten."

He tipped the brim of his hat back. "That's a big statement since my mother makes the best apple pie on the planet."

"I really like Cora Lee," she said, "but I'll put my pies up against hers anytime."

"Well," Jesse said nodding, "now there's no choice. You have to come over so we can settle this."

She chewed at her bottom lip for a second before saying, "Okay. For a few minutes. Then I've got to get Mac and head home. I'm later than I thought I'd be, but I wanted to finish the pie so I could bring it to you."

The first raindrops plopped into the dirt as they climbed the steps to the stone porch. Jesse opened the heavily carved front door and stood back to allow Jillian to enter first.

He watched her as she looked around and Jesse saw his place through her eyes. Wide plank, golden oak floors, Native American paintings and family photos on the walls and Navajo rugs scattered across the floors. She wandered through the entryway, peeked into the main room, and he knew she saw a completely masculine space. Well, hell, he lived here alone, so why would there be feminine touches? The only women who ever came into his house were his mother and sister and the housekeeper, once a week. When Jesse wanted a woman he went to her place.

He never brought them to the ranch. To this house. He didn't want some woman to start feeling cozy in his place. Start leaving bits of clothing or makeup or whatever, trying to stake a claim both on him and his world.

This was different, though, he assured himself. Jillian wouldn't be here long. As much as he'd like to, he wouldn't be steering her down the hall to his room and laying her out across his bed. Gritting his teeth, he pushed that thought away and watched her. She looked around the main room and he saw it fresh, through her.

Burgundy-colored leather chairs and couches were grouped in front of a stone fireplace that was perfect when it was cold enough for a fire. Thank God he had a housekeeper, so the place wasn't covered in an inch of dust, but there were books stacked on tables, an abandoned coffee cup and invoices, records and bills scattered on the floor around the chair he usually sat in.

"It's a great place," she said, taking in the wide windows that overlooked the corral and the ranch yard. Then her gaze landed on the paperwork. "Interesting filing system."

"Yeah." He pulled his hat off and set it, crown down, on the closest table. "I was working when Carlos came to get me to ride out to the pasture and check on a few of the herd. We've got some pregnant cows out there and wanted to make sure they had enough water."

"I thought you had ponds and lakes."

"We do," he said, "but sometimes, the stock ponds get gummed up or start going dry."

"How do you keep track of so many animals?"

He shrugged. "The cowboys ride the land most days, we keep a running head count of the cattle so if any wander off, we can go find 'em."

"So you're riding across the ranch every day?"

"I wish," he muttered, then glanced at the paperwork. "If I had my way, yeah. But there's a lot of that to be done, too. Plus there's more than the animals to care for. There are stock ponds to keep clean and clear, feed fields to manage and the pastures themselves."

She shook her head. "It sounds intimidating."

"Can be," he agreed, and realized this was the first time a woman had actually asked him about his work. And she looked as though she really was interested. "If you don't learn from the best. I did. My dad knew everything there was to know about ranching and he taught me."

"From everything Lucy and Cora Lee have told me about him, he sounds like a very special man."

"He was. In every way." Jesse stared out the front window at the ranch he'd loved from the first moment he'd set foot on the place. "He loved Lucy and me and raised us as if we were his own."

Nodding, she turned, too, to look out the window at the darkness creeping in as twilight ended. "That is special. Not everyone can accept a child other than their own."

"Yeah, well," he said, "Roy was one of a kind." To change the subject, he pulled the foil back from the pie and took a whiff. "Smells good."

"Tastes better." A couple of long, silent seconds ticked past, then she said abruptly, "Have you always wanted to be a rancher?"

"For as long as I can remember." He took her arm and steered her down the long hall toward the back of the house. "Let's get to the kitchen so I can grab a fork."

They walked through the dining room, past a wide table long enough to seat twelve comfortably and through a door into the kitchen. Beside him, Jillian stopped dead, gasped in astonishment, then turned a slow circle, looking all around.

"What is it?"

She held up one hand for silence and murmured, "Just, wait. I'm having a moment here."

Her features told him she loved the room. The walls were a soft blue, cabinets were white and the countertops were black granite. In front of the bay window was a round pedestal table and matching chairs where Jesse usually ate since the dining room was too huge for a man alone. The appliances were all top-of-the-line stainless steel. Over the built-in gas stove was a copper range hood and in the middle island was a second sink and Jesse's favorite part of the kitchen, an indoor grill.

"This is...amazing." Her voice was low and breathy, as if she were in church. She took a step farther into the room, reached out one hand and stroked her fingertips across the black granite. Looking back at him, she said, "I have serious kitchen envy. What I could do with— It's a dream kitchen. Like something you'd see in a magazine."

He chuckled, moved past her and set the pie down on the center island. Yanking open a drawer, he pulled out two forks. "Glad you like it. And it's funny you should say that about a magazine kitchen. That's exactly what this was."

"What do you mean?"

He turned to a cupboard, took down two plates

and then grabbed a pie slicer from another drawer. "When I was building this place, Lucy showed me a picture of this exact kitchen in a magazine. So I showed it to the architect and told him I wanted it."

She blinked at him and laughed a little. "I don't think I've ever known anyone who would—or could—do that."

He shrugged. "It's a kitchen. Don't really use it all that much, except to make coffee and to keep my beer cold."

"Oh, God…"

He looked up when she moaned. "The best part of the whole kitchen, to my mind, is the grill there. Most times when I come in at the end of the day I'm too tired to cook, but I can always grill. Toss a steak on there and I'm good."

"That's practically criminal," she said softly.

"What?" He looked at her.

"To have this fantastic kitchen and only use the island grill?" She shook her head again. "Criminal."

"Well, don't arrest me until I've tried the pie." He cut two slices, plated them, then carried both plates to the table. "Come on. If you don't have some I'll wonder if you poisoned it or something."

She followed and sat opposite him. Outside, twilight lay across the ranch and shimmered on the raindrops pelting the window. Within minutes, darkness would drop like a curtain. "I would never ruin one of my pies with poison."

He grinned. "Good to know."

It felt good, sitting there with her in the dying light. Talking with her. Seeing her smile. Lust still clawed at his insides, but there was another part of him that was enjoying this moment. "Okay," he said, lifting his fork. "Moment of truth."

"I'm not worried."

"Confident," he said. "I like it."

He took a bite of the pie and the minute it hit his tongue, Jesse groaned quietly. Spices exploded in his mouth, combining into flavors like he'd never tasted before. He chewed, swallowed, then took another bite.

She grinned. "Told you."

When he could, Jesse said, "You're a witch or something, right? This is incredible. Seriously great."

She seemed to practically glow under his compliments and he had to wonder about that. "Thank you," she said, taking a bite of the pie herself. "It's my grandma Rhonda's recipe. She taught me."

"Like I said earlier, it's all about learning from the best."

Her smile widened. "She really was, too. The best, I mean."

"Got to see a lot of her when you were a kid?"

"She raised me," Jillian said simply in a tone that told him she wouldn't welcome questions.

He could live with that. "Well, she did a damn good job of it as far as I can see."

"Thanks."

"You should sell these," Jesse told her, wolfing down another bite of pie.

"That's the plan."

He stopped. "Is that right?"

Nodding, she said, "I love baking and I'm good at it."

"I can testify."

"I want to open a shop. Pies. Cookies. Cakes." She paused as if she'd heard the excitement in her own voice and was embarrassed by it. "Well, that's the dream anyway."

"With talent like this, it should be more than a dream."

She smiled and in the dim light, he thought he saw her eyes sparkling. Reaching back behind him, Jesse hit the switch for the overhead light. It was on a dimmer switch, so a soft glow settled over the table and the two people seated there.

"That's nice." She looked up at the rustic/industrial chandelier with glass spheres and curved iron arms.

"Yeah. Before dawn I don't like being stabbed in the eye with light while I drink my coffee."

She laughed a little and that low, throaty sound did some amazing things to his insides.

"So," he asked, "why're you working at the day care when you can cook like this?"

She shrugged. "I needed a job. Besides, I don't have enough money yet to get a pie shop going."

"How much do you have?" Jesse didn't know why he was asking, other than that he wanted to see that excited gleam in her eyes again.

She looked as if she was going to refuse to answer and he couldn't blame her. Kind of a rude question. But then she took a breath and sighed. "When I sold my grandmother's mobile home a few years ago, I got fifteen thousand, but I'll need more than that. So I've been saving and in a few years, I should be able to do it."

He took another bite of the truly great pie and chewed thoughtfully. "We own half of Royal, you know."

"Congratulations."

"Not what I meant." He waved his fork at her. "I think I know a shop on Main Street that would work for you."

She gasped, clearly stunned, and he enjoyed the moment before she spoke. "Thanks, but like I said, I'll need more start-up capital to—"

"The shop's already set up with what you'd need. Used to be a bakery until the owner moved to Michigan for some reason…"

Her fingers tapped on the tabletop and he could see her thinking, wondering, worrying.

"But—"

"And if you need more capital, I can advance it to you."

"Absolutely not." She shook her head, squared her shoulders and sat so straight in her chair, it was as if she had a board stuffed down the back of her shirt. "The Sanders family has already set me up in an apartment. I took that because Mac needed it. But I don't do charity."

"Good," he said roughly, keeping his voice stern and businesslike. "Because that's not what I'm offering. I'll be your partner."

Six

Jillian just stared at him. She couldn't believe what she was hearing. How had she gone from bringing Jesse a pie to him offering to set her up in business? And why was she even considering this?

"Silent partner," he added quickly and took another bite of pie. "I'll back you and when the shop's up and going, you can pay me back. Buy me out."

Excitement shot through her, but she quickly stamped it out, as she would hot sparks before they could start a forest fire. She couldn't do this. Jesse as a *partner*? Hadn't she been telling herself to see *less* of him? Even if he was a silent partner, she would have to work with him. A lot.

Oh, why was she even considering this? It was crazy. Impossible. "It could take years to pay you back," she said, firmly shaking her head.

"Not if you're selling pies like this." Jesse waved the fork at her. "Once people taste what you can do, you'll be so busy it'll make your head spin. The solid truth here is, you make a hell of a pie."

That idea made her smile and everything in her yearned. Jillian had had this dream of her own shop for so many years now. And since Mac's birth, the dream had become more fierce. She wanted to have her own business, make her own rules, live her own life and show her baby girl that you could do anything if you were willing to work for it.

She hadn't expected this. Didn't have a response ready. Maybe she should have said "no" right off the bat. But the thought of making her dream a reality years sooner than she'd hoped was too tempting to dismiss offhand. Still, she had to know. Understand.

"I don't get it," she said softly, tipping her head to one side as she watched him, trying to gauge what he was thinking. "Why would you want to do this?"

"Do I need a reason?"

She laughed shortly. "Well, yes."

"Fine." He sat back in his chair and studied her in the golden glow of the overhead lamp. "I figure if you can bake a pie like *this* in that tiny excuse for a kitchen in the apartment—there's no telling what you could pull off with the room to grow."

"Hmm."

"This is a straight-up business deal," he said, and Jillian met his shadowed gaze. "We'll have the family lawyers draw up the paperwork—"

"I don't know..." She laid one hand against her belly in a futile attempt to ease the butterflies racing around inside. This was all happening so fast she couldn't be sure about what to do. But in the next instant, Jillian told herself that this was the chance she'd been waiting, hoping for. Did it matter that Jesse was helping her? Again? Once she paid him back, the business would be hers completely, and wasn't that what was really important?

As if sensing that she was waffling, Jesse looked into her eyes and said, "The shop on Main has most of what you'd need. Anything else required we can get. Have you set up and running inside a month if you want it."

"A month." She could have her own shop in a *month.* Jillian took a deep breath and held it, hoping to steady the nerves, the questions, rattling her. It didn't help. *A month.* All she had to do was forego her pride and accept Jesse's offer. But was it pride keeping her from accepting his help? Didn't other businesses have investors? Why shouldn't she?

"Or sooner," he tempted.

Sooner. She chewed at her bottom lip and mentally raced through the colliding thoughts in her mind. The pros. The cons. The temptations and dangers of being too close to Jesse Navarro. About giving up the very essence of herself—her self-reliance. Since she was a child when her parents disappeared from her life, Jillian had learned to count on *herself.* Her grandmother had taught her to go for what she wanted but to never expect someone else to get it for her.

She'd worked and saved and maybe in another year or two, she could pull off opening her own shop under her own power. Sure, she'd still have needed a business loan, but she would have taken as little as she could because the thought of being in debt was terrifying. But if she was willing to bend, she could have that dream much sooner than she could have imagined. All she had to do was get past the life lessons that had guided her for so long.

Really, what was wrong with his offer? She wasn't really giving anything up. She would still do the work and build the business on her own. It was as if she were getting a loan from a bank. Only this bank happened to be gorgeous and starring nightly in her dreams.

As Jillian considered everything, her mind a whirlwind of disjointed thoughts, she realized something. She wanted to do this. Why should she wait years to have what she could have now? Self-reliance would still be her mainstay as it would be up to *her* whether her shop was a success or not. She wouldn't lose anything by accepting Jesse's offer. Instead, she could take a stand and start building the future.

Then she considered Mac in all of this. Her baby girl. Jillian wanted so much for her. If she waited until she'd saved all the money she might need, it could be two or three more years before she could open a shop. And that meant it might be years before she could find a bigger apartment—or a house—and she wanted that for Mac. Her little girl deserved to have her own yard to play in. She'd seen Mac with Brody, here on the ranch where the kids had room to run and play and make all the noise they wanted to without worrying about upsetting the person in the next apartment.

If she accepted Jesse's help, she'd be able to put her dreams on the fast track and that meant a better life for Mac. Wasn't that what coming to Texas in the first place had been all about?

"I can practically hear you thinking," Jesse said wryly.

"It's a lot to think about," she admitted and watched him savor another bite of pie.

"Not so much really," he said and set his fork down. "You've got talent and a plan. I can help you with getting started on that plan. Pretty straightforward."

"When you put it like that, sure," she said.

"So is that a yes?"

Jillian looked into his eyes and knew she was

going to say *yes.* If there was still some hesitation inside her, she could understand it, but she wouldn't let it sway her. Maybe it was just time to throw caution to the wind and take the chance being offered. She took a breath, held his gaze and took the plunge. "I think so."

"Good." A smile lit up his eyes as he reached one hand across the table. "Well, then. Before you can change your mind, shake on it."

Steadying herself, Jillian slipped her hand into his and tried not to notice how her skin sizzled and burned at the contact. Electricity hummed up her arm to bounce around her chest like a crazed ping-pong ball. He squeezed her hand. "I'll call the lawyers tomorrow morning."

Nodding, she took a breath and said, "Okay."

He let her go and for a second, Jillian really missed the feel of his much bigger hand wrapped around hers. That was probably not what she should be thinking about a business partner.

"You're not going to change your mind, are you?"

She looked at him and shook her head. "No. Decisions are hard, but once they're made, that's it."

"Good to know." He glanced at the piece of pie on her plate. "You going to finish that?"

Jillian laughed and felt the butterflies settle. She handed her plate over and said, "I only hope the rest of Royal likes my pies as much as you do."

His dark eyes locked onto hers. His voice dropped to a husky murmur. "You can count on it."

They were talking about the pie shop, but there was an undercurrent, as well. What else could she count on? Jillian wondered. And why were her insides jumping again?

"Mama!" An eager shout echoed through the house.

Jillian blew out a breath and smiled. The tension between them shattered completely and then another voice shouted and the shared moment was over.

"Uncle Jesse!" Brody's voice.

"Hey, you guys!" Lucy called out an instant later. "Mac saw your car here and we came to find you!"

Jesse sighed a little. "Guess we're done talking about this for now. Good thing we came to an agreement already." Then he yelled, "In the kitchen."

She smiled at the sound of both kids clattering down the hall toward them. "Let me know what the lawyers say."

"Absolutely."

An instant later, both kids ran into the kitchen in a burst of noise and color—they were laughing in delight at their race down the hall. Lucy was right behind them.

"Wow," she said with a knowing smile as she strolled into the kitchen, "this looks…cozy. Something tells me we showed up too early."

"Not at all," Jillian said, scooping her daughter

into her arms as she got to her feet. "I was just about to come to your house to get Mac."

"Uh-huh." Lucy's smile didn't fade, but her eyebrows lifted as she studied first Jillian, then Jesse.

Jillian fired off a narrow-eyed look at her friend and wasn't surprised when Lucy unapologetically winked at her.

"Oh, what's this?" she crowed when she spotted the pie on the counter. "God, I love pie." Lucy grabbed a fork from the drawer and went for a bite. "This is amazing," she said, already dipping in for another bite. "Jillian, did you *make* this?"

"I wanted to thank Jesse for all of his help, so yes. I baked it this afternoon."

"Boy, when you want to thank *me* for something, my favorite is lemon meringue." Lucy went for another taste, but Jesse smacked her hand away.

"Get your own pie."

"Hmm. Territorial. Interesting." She shrugged, licked her fork, then looked from one to the other of them. "You know, I'm really glad you're both here together because I need to ask a favor."

Jillian was wary. It hadn't taken her long to know when her friend was up to something. "What?"

"Oh," Lucy said, reaching over to smooth Brody's hair back from his forehead, "you know the gala at the TCC? Well, I've got tickets to go, but I just don't feel right about it."

"Lucy..."

She ignored Jillian and focused on her brother. "I mean, Jillian's new in town and she's been working so hard, this would be a great way for her to meet people *and* have some fun for a change."

Jesse looked at Jillian and knew the woman was torn between wanting to go and wanting his sister to be quiet. Normally, he didn't do the formal get-togethers at the club. He was most at home in his jeans, a work shirt and worn boots, riding a horse, being out under the sky. Jesse didn't care much for spending an entire evening suffering through wearing a tux. But damned if he didn't want to see Jillian all dressed up. Watching her now, he could see how irritated she must be toward his sister. That he could completely sympathize with. But Lucy had a point, too.

"I don't need a night of fun," Jillian argued.

"Oh, please." His sister glanced back at her. "You proved how much you need one today. You were supposed to go and relax for a while and instead you made a pie. A great pie, but come on. Baking is not relaxing."

"It is for me," Jillian said.

Lucy sighed dramatically. "Jillian, everyone needs fun once in a while. Even the great Stone Face here, right Jesse?"

"What's a stone face?" Brody asked.

"Never mind," Jesse said, giving his sister a look

that he gave her every time she was after something. It had never worked, but he kept trying.

"I really don't have anything to wear," Jillian was saying as a last-ditch attempt to make Lucy drop it.

Jesse could have told her the attempt was futile.

"Oh, this year it's called the Black and White Ball. We'll go shopping." Lucy whipped back around to look meaningfully at Jesse.

He got the message and for whatever reason, he found it didn't bother him at all to say, "So, Jillian. Want to go to the ball with me?"

Jillian kissed Mac, glared at Lucy, then shifted her gaze to Jesse again. He knew when he saw the shine in her eyes that she was going to agree, but he liked hearing her say, "I'd love to."

"Excellent," Lucy announced and immediately launched into plans for shopping, getting Jillian's hair and nails done, and while his sister talked, Jesse watched Jillian—the excitement in her eyes, the smile curving her mouth, the way her shirt clung to her breasts—and he fervently wished his sister was anywhere else.

The following day was Jillian's day off and true to her word, Lucy showed up at the apartment to pick up her and Mac. They dropped the kids off at the TCC day care for a few hours and hit the Courtyard shops. Most of the stores were no more than booths sectioned off inside a huge red barn that used to be part of a working ranch. But the land was sold, and some enterprising soul had turned the barn and several outbuildings into an eclectic shopping center.

Jillian normally guarded her bank account like a miser. But going to this black-tie gala, she couldn't exactly attend in jeans, so she was determined to treat herself. And the one dressy outfit she had with her had been fine for Will's memorial, but would be completely out of place at a gala. How long had it been since she had been on an actual date? Not that this was a date, really. Jesse was just doing his sister a favor and Jillian wasn't reading anything into it at all, but that didn't mean she couldn't look great, did it?

"It's a black-and-white ball this year," Lucy reminded her as they entered the boutique. "So no red dresses, which is a damn shame if you ask me, because you probably look great in red."

The shop was in one of the outbuildings near the barn itself and it was pretty without being intimidating. Beautiful clothes hung in groups of color and style. The walls were a pale yellow and there were baskets of live plants and vases of flowers scattered throughout the room.

"My Valkyrie uniform was red," Jillian told her, "so trust me when I say I'm okay with going for black or white."

Lucy shook her head and her layered brown hair swung around her face with the motion. "I really want to see that uniform. But for now… Ooh. Look at *that*."

Jillian followed in Lucy's wake and she felt both eyebrows arch at first sight of the dress. "I don't know," she said warily. "There's not a lot of fabric there."

Lucy sighed dramatically. "What are you, eighty? You've got a great figure, why not flaunt it? Knock Jesse off his feet."

Jillian eyed her friend suspiciously. "That's not what this is about."

"No, of course not," her friend cooed, lifting the hanger off the rack to further admire the really tiny dress. "But it couldn't hurt to make his eyeballs pop out, could it?"

Jillian thought about that for a second and if she was going to be honest with herself, she had to admit that it would be fun to make Jesse's jaw drop when he saw her. So far, he'd only seen her in jeans, with Mac or with the other kids at the day care.

"You could at least try it on after all the trouble I went to find it," Lucy urged, waving the dress back and forth as if trying to hypnotize her friend into submission.

Jillian laughed. "It's the first store we've been to and the first dress you saw."

"Oh, don't be logical." Lucy pushed the dress into Jillian's hands. "Just try it on while I look for more."

Sighing a little at the futility of actually winning

an argument with her friend, Jillian carried the dress to the counter and a woman there opened a changing room for her. In a few minutes, she was wearing what little fabric there was and wondering if she could be arrested.

"Well?" Lucy asked from outside the door.

"My old uniform covered more."

Lucy laughed. "Come on, let me see."

Opening the door, Jillian stepped out and stopped in front of a full-length mirror. She tugged the hem of the slightly full skirt down, but it stopped midthigh no matter what she did. She pulled the bodice up, but it remained in place, displaying breasts that hadn't seen the light of day in more than a year.

She looked over her shoulder into the mirror and swore she could see the dimples at the top of her butt, the back was cut so low. "Oh, I don't think—"

"It's *perfect*," Lucy said breathlessly as she handed the three other dresses she'd brought just in case, over to the clerk. "We won't need these."

Jillian's head whipped up. "No, wait, I should—"

"Buy some sky-high black heels, wear your hair down and ooh, we should get you some black lingerie while we're out, too." Lucy slapped her hands together and scrubbed her palms. "Isn't this *fun*?"

"Lucy, I don't know about this..."

Her friend stepped up behind her and met Jillian's gaze in the mirror. "My brother's eyes are going to do more than pop. They'll probably jump out of his head and roll across the floor."

Jillian laughed, then tugged at the hem again. "There's an image."

Lucy slapped her hands down. "Stop tugging. You look amazing. Just enjoy it."

She half turned in front of the mirror, examining herself from every angle. The dress *did* look good on her. It was just that there was so little of it. Then she thought about what Lucy had said about Jesse's reaction. Jillian told herself that shouldn't matter, but she knew she was lying.

Of course it mattered. She might not want a permanent man—because so far, in her experience, men hadn't *been* permanent at all—but a temporary man might be just the thing. She'd spent so many nights dreaming about Jesse, wanting him, wouldn't it be better to just *have* him? Once the sexual tension was eased, she could get past this, right? Focus on her life, her daughter, her future.

They'd just reached an agreement. They were going to be partners. But if this incredible sexual tension remained between them, working together wouldn't be easy. So really, sleeping with Jesse would be the smart thing to do. *Oh, that was just a really sad attempt at justification.*

"Well?" Lucy asked from behind her. "What's the decision?"

Jillian looked her friend in the eye. "Where do we find me sky-high black heels?"

Lucy grinned.

Two hours later, they were both exhausted, and stopped at the Courtyard café for coffee and muffins. The sky was clear and sharply blue. The sun was shining and already warm, but in the shade, they didn't mind the growing heat as much.

Jillian should have been feeling guilty. She'd dropped a lot of money today on lingerie, shoes and a dress she couldn't imagine wearing more than once. And then there was the mani/pedi Lucy had talked her into. Still a little shocked, she whispered, "I can't believe I spent all that money."

"It's an investment," Lucy assured her and broke off a piece of blueberry muffin.

Laughing, Jillian asked, "In *what*?"

"Yourself, silly." Lucy leaned on the tabletop. "You're going to meet a lot of people at the gala. And when you've got your pie shop open, they'll all come and buy delicious goodies from you."

Wryly, Jillian said, "Because of the black dress."

Lucy grinned again. "Can't hurt. Besides, don't you deserve a treat once in a while, Jill? You don't mind if I call you Jill, do you?"

"No." She smiled. "My grandmother always did."

"Good. So anyway, Jill, you look fabulous and Jesse will introduce you around and you'll make a big splash."

"Uh-huh."

"Oh," Lucy added as if an afterthought, "I was thinking that maybe the night of the dance, why don't we just have Mac spend the night at my place?"

"Why?" Suspicious, she watched her friend warily.

"Well, you'll be getting in late," Lucy said, lifting her coffee cup for a sip. "You don't want to wake her up just to take her home and put her to bed again, do you?"

"I guess not, but…" Cocking her head to one side, Jillian watched Lucy feign all innocence for a minute or two. "I get the feeling I'm being set up."

"That's because you're a very smart woman."

"Lucy…"

"Oh, relax already." The other woman took another bite of her muffin. "There's no big conspiracy or anything. We're friends. I'm just helping out."

"Uh-huh." Jillian wasn't convinced. "Lucy, this is really sweet of you, I think, but I don't want a man in my life."

"How about in your bed?"

"My— We're talking about your brother here."

"Yes and believe it or not," Lucy said in a whisper, "I know that my brothers have sex. The lucky bastards. I haven't had sex in too long to think about but that's not the point at the moment."

"What is the point?"

"That I've seen the way you and Jesse look at each other. Heck, the air between you practically sizzles."

Jillian took a breath. Lucy was right. She'd been feeling it for weeks now and there didn't seem any reason to deny it. "That doesn't mean—"

"It means, you're grown-ups. You clearly like each other. Obviously, you *want* each other. So, why not?"

"And this isn't about matchmaking?"

Lucy slapped one hand to her chest in mock outrage. "Would I do that?"

"Yes," Jillian said, laughing.

"Okay," Lucy admitted, unrepentant. "I would. But I'm not. I'm just paving the way to a little recreational sex." She sighed. "Just because I'm living like a vestal virgin doesn't mean you have to."

Jillian thought about it while Lucy went in to get them refills. This wasn't about love. She *did* like Jesse. A lot. And boy, did she want him. One night didn't have to lead to forever. Especially since forever just didn't exist outside novels. But one night could be something special she'd always remember.

When Lucy came back with fresh coffee, she asked, "So? Does Mac spend the night with me?"

"Yes." Nodding, Jillian said, "Just don't expect something to come of this because it's not going to."

"Jill, the truth is, I want to see my brother happy. I want to see my friend happy." Lucy shrugged. "Is that so bad?"

"No, it's not. And I really do appreciate the thought, Lucy, but I'm just not looking for love."

Lucy smiled. "Oh, sweetie, that's exactly when you usually find it."

Seven

The more Jesse thought about attending the gala with Jillian, the more he was worried she might get the wrong idea. She wasn't the kind of woman to be with for a night and then dismiss. She was a *mother*, for God's sake. His sister's friend. And now she was going to be his business partner.

No way he could be as cavalier with Jillian as he always had been with the other women who had come and gone from his life in a blur. But he couldn't offer her more, either. So what the hell was he doing?

Jesse walked into the main house, intending to dump all of this on his younger brother and see what Will thought about it all. Truth be told, he needed someone else's input. His own brain had been chewing on the problem of Jillian for weeks and he was still tied up in knots.

But at the threshold of the great room, Jesse stopped dead. Will wasn't alone. If he'd been paying attention, Jesse would have seen the strange car parked outside the house. As it was, seeing Megan Phillips Sanders sitting on a couch beside Will caught Jesse off guard.

His brother and the woman he was legally married to were looking at a photo album and hadn't noticed his arrival.

"Looks like it was a nice wedding," Will said, flipping through pages.

"I thought so at the time," Megan said. "I thought it was romantic that you—I mean *he*—wanted the ceremony to be on a beach, just the two of us. Looking back, I feel like an idiot."

"You shouldn't," Will told her. "I'm the idiot who trusted Rich, gave him the room he needed to steal my life and to trick you."

Megan laughed shortly. "You notice how we're both blaming ourselves and *not* blaming the one person who deserves the blame?"

When Will smiled in response, Jesse was relieved to see it. There hadn't been many of those smiles since Will came home. Maybe Megan and Will could help each other through the mess that Rich had left in his wake.

"Oh, I blame Rich all right," Will assured her. "And I'm going to do everything I can to make sure he's caught and thrown into jail for a hundred years."

Megan took the photo album and closed it with a slap. "That'd be good."

Jesse was beginning to feel like some Peeping Tom, so he stepped into the room and said hello.

"Jesse, hello," Megan said. She was a pretty woman with bright blue eyes, brown and gold hair, and she always looked like she'd stepped out of a magazine. Her clothes, shoes and purse always matched. Jesse had no idea how women did that.

"Didn't mean to interrupt," Jesse said.

"You're not," Will told him. "We were just talking. Megan was showing me pictures of her wedding to—well, *me*, I guess."

Megan sighed. "Not you. I know that now. Wish I had known then."

Jesse nodded. "We're all feeling that way, Megan."

"You're being very nice."

"None of this is your fault," Will told her.

Jesse thought that Will looked more relaxed than Jesse had seen him in the last several weeks and for that, the Sanders family owed Megan.

To Jesse, Will said, "I was just telling Megan that I have to put up with house arrest and she has to keep up the pretense of our marriage if we want to catch Rich and throw him into the deepest, dankest cell the law can find."

"I don't think that's a word, but I'm with you. And yeah," Jesse said, shifting to look at Megan. "I'm sorry about that. Got to be hard on you pretending to care about the man who lied to you."

She smoothed her palms over the black knee-length skirt she wore. "It's not, really. Rich is gone and I don't know if he even intends to come back this time. Don't know how he could, really, since everyone thinks Will Sanders is dead. But either way," she added, looking at Will, "everyone I know was used to you—I mean *him*—being gone on business a lot, so I just smile and nod when people ask about my husband."

"You're being really great about all of this," Will said.

"If I throw a fit, will it help?"

He grinned. "No."

"Well, then, why bother, right?" Megan rose and picked up her purse from the table. "I've really got to get going now. But if it's all right with you, I'd like to come back. Talk with you again, Will. About Rich and well…just all of it."

He stood up and took her hand. "I'd like that, too. Feels like the two of us are sharing a leaky canoe. I think teamwork is required."

Megan smiled at him. Jesse noticed the sparkle in her eyes and wondered if Will had seen it, too.

"If it's okay, I'll come back tomorrow and we can talk about what the plan is going forward."

"Sure. That's great." Will walked her to the door, the two of them passing close to Jesse.

"It was nice to see you," Megan said.

"You, too, Megan," Jesse answered.

"Be right back," Will said.

Jesse wandered toward the cold stone hearth and waited for his brother to see Megan off. So the two of them had been looking at a wedding album. Damn. That had to have hit Will like a truck. He couldn't even imagine what it was like for him to look at wedding pictures featuring the man who'd tried to kill him pretending to *be* him.

And what must Megan be feeling about all of this? She'd married a man who'd turned out to be nothing but smoke and mirrors. Now she was married to a *different* man with the same name. Jesse was beginning to think Royal, Texas, was the playground of some really annoying gods.

"Man, that was rough," Will said as he walked back into the room. He dropped down into a chair and stared up at Jesse. "I took your suggestion. This morning, I called Megan, invited her out to the ranch and when she got here, I shut up and let her talk. She told me everything from her point of view. I wouldn't have believed it possible, but now I want to beat Rich senseless even more than I did before."

Jesse perched on the arm of a chair opposite his brother. "How's she doing?"

"Oh, great." Sarcasm colored his tone. "She's

married to a stranger, just like I am. What's that old TV show we used to watch in marathons?"

"Twilight Zone," Jesse provided.

"That's it. And that's where I'm living." Will shook his head, then scrubbed one hand across his eyes. "What's life like in the real world?"

"Confusing as hell."

Will's eyebrows arched. "Good. Tell me. Give me something to focus on that's *not* me."

Jesse snorted and pushed up from the chair. Stalking to the fireplace, he laid one hand on the mantel and leaned in, wishing it was cold enough to have a damn fire. There was something soothing about the snap and hiss of flames over logs. "Apparently, I'm not only going to back Jillian in a pie shop, but I'm taking her to the TCC gala."

Will shook his head. "Say again. Slower."

So Jesse told him everything and realized as he did how much he'd missed being able to bounce things off Will. During that time when Rich was usurping Will's life, he'd pretty much cut himself off from the family. Of course now Jesse could look back and see exactly why. The impostor couldn't risk spending too much time with the Sanders family because they might have seen through the masquerade. At the time, he'd resented Will for putting their mother and sister through so much pain. Now, he was just grateful to have his brother back.

"So the pie was good, huh? Did you save me any?"

"Figures that's what you took out of everything I just said." Jesse shook his head. Had he just been thinking how good it was to be able to talk to the man?

"I'm hungry. Shoot me." Will grinned and gave his brother a long look. "I'm glad you're going to help Jillian out with the shop."

"Yeah?"

"Yeah. Rich pulled her into all of this then walked away. I figure the Sanders family owes her."

Nodding, Jesse said, "That's how I felt."

"But the gala thing..." Will's grin widened. "I've never known you to do something you didn't want to do. So—"

"I don't want to go to the damn dance," Jesse assured him. "What I want is *her* and that's not okay."

"Why the hell not?"

Jesse straightened up then scrubbed both hands across his face. "Because she's not the kind of woman for an uncomplicated affair and I'm not looking for anything else."

"Again I ask," Will said, "why not?"

"Seriously?" Jesse just stared at him. "You were here when Lucy's husband died, Will."

"What's Dane's death got to do with—" he broke off and sighed. "Guilt. Is that what this is about? You think you don't get something because you're not through paying your debt to some otherworldly fate?"

"Dane died because of me," Jesse ground out.

Will scowled at him and snapped, "He died because a horse trampled him."

"He was helping *me*."

"Because he asked you to teach him." Will stood up and faced his brother. "He wanted to fit in on the ranch. He wanted to be a part of it all and you obliged him. Not your damn fault that stallion went crazy."

He wished he could believe that, but Jesse knew different. He never should have allowed Dane into the corral with that horse. It was too wild, and he had been too inexperienced.

"I shouldn't have let him get so close."

"Hard to learn from a distance."

"Our nephew doesn't have a father because of decisions I made."

"Believe it or not, Jesse, you are *not* the center of the universe. Fate, Karma, whatever, doesn't revolve around whatever it is you're doing from day to day."

"Brody's father is *dead*. Nothing you say can change that."

Still scowling, Will reminded him, "Brody has two uncles, a grandmother and a mom who's nuts about him. That's more than a lot of kids have."

Facts didn't seem to ease the regret and guilt that could still rise up and choke him without a moment's warning. Just the other day, he'd watched Brody riding his first pony and thought that Dane should be there, seeing his son grow. Instead, the man had died, never even knowing that Lucy was pregnant.

"You're just determined to wear a hair shirt and beat yourself over the head with this, aren't you?"

Jesse shot his brother a hard glare. "For a while there, I was glad to have you to talk to again. Not so sure, now."

Will smiled. "If you're just looking for someone to agree with you, talk to yourself."

"Thanks. Helpful."

"You want helpful? Here it is." Will dropped into his chair again, stretched his legs out in front of him and crossed his feet at the ankle. "Go to the dance. Kiss that woman. Don't be an idiot, and take her to bed if she'll have you. Let yourself live again, Jesse. Because from where I'm sitting, it looks like I'm not the only one on house arrest."

The night of the gala, Jillian was as nervous as a teenager on her first date. "Silly." She looked at her reflection in the bathroom mirror and hardly recognized herself. She hadn't really bothered to fix her hair and take care with her makeup since Cora Lee had hosted that service for Will a few weeks ago. And that had really been more casual-dressy. This was something else entirely. And she hadn't worn anything so blatantly feminine since she quit her job and retired her Valkyrie uniform.

Anxious, she smoothed her hands down over the front of her dress and wondered *again* if she'd done the right thing buying it. Sure, it looked good on her, but maybe it would send the wrong signals to Jesse. They were going to be business partners so they should keep things platonic.

"Yeah, this dress does not say 'Be my friend,'" she said, frowning. "It's screaming 'Take me, I'm yours.'"

At that thought she slapped both hands to her middle and forced deep breaths into her lungs. Mac was at Lucy's, and Jillian knew she didn't have to worry about her girl. Mac had been so excited to have a sleepover with Brody she'd forgotten to kiss her mommy goodbye.

"And that's a good thing," she assured her reflection.

Jillian made another adjustment to her hair, lying in soft waves down her back. Having her hair loose made her feel a little better about how much skin was displayed by the deeply cut back of the dress.

When the knock on the door sounded, she jumped, then laughed at herself. "Get a grip, Jillian." She checked the fall of the short, slightly full skirt, then resolutely left the bathroom.

Still nervous, she opened the door and simply stared. Jesse. Like he stepped out of a dream. Tall and gorgeous, the man had been born to wear a tuxedo. He might not be pleased about it, but Jesse was gorgeous. In his elegantly tailored tux, with a crisp white shirt and black bow tie, he looked as if he should be on the cover of *GQ*. Of course, you couldn't take the ranch out of the man completely. He wore shining black boots and a black cowboy hat that only added to the whole picture that was taking her breath away. "You look very handsome."

"I don't know about that," he said, "but you look beautiful."

The way he was looking at her—as if he could simply gobble her up—made her *feel* beautiful. And it made her feel other things, as well. Things she'd been trying desperately not to think about. But with the heat in his gaze as he looked at her, those thoughts roared into life and refused to be pushed aside. She took a breath to steady herself. "Thank you. Why don't you come in? I'll get my purse and wrap."

Stepping past her into the apartment, Jesse stopped and stared at the room in front of him. Jillian smiled at the stunned expression on his face.

"Look a little different in here?" she asked unnecessarily.

He glanced at her briefly and grinned. "I wouldn't have believed it."

Jillian looked at the apartment and gave a short sigh of satisfaction. The walls were now a soft green. There were framed photos from magazines of places she one day wanted to visit on the walls and a few brightly colored rugs she'd found at the consignment shop on the floor. She'd made a room divider from two old doors she'd found at a garage sale and used it to block her bed from the rest of the room. It was still small, of course, but now it had personality. It was home. Hers and Mac's.

"I can't believe you did all of this. It looks great."

"Thanks." She picked up her small, black bag and swung the rose-colored wrap Lucy had loaned her over her shoulders.

Jesse looked her up and down again and said, "You keep surprising me."

"Is that bad?" she asked, meeting his gaze.

"No. I like surprises."

The look in his eyes sent heat sizzling across her skin. Jillian took a breath and relished the burn. What he could do to her with his eyes was like nothing she'd ever experienced before. "Me, too."

His eyes flashed. "Good to know."

Oh, boy. She turned for the door. He grabbed her upper arm, spun her around and pulled her in tightly to him.

"Surprise," he whispered just before he bent his head and took her mouth with the kind of hunger that vanquished anything that stood in its way.

At the first touch of his mouth, Jillian gasped, then sighed, lifting her arms to hook them around his neck. He parted her lips with his tongue and she welcomed it, tangling her tongue with his in a seductive dance that had her heart hammering in her chest and her blood rushing through her veins.

She felt a burning ache awaken deep inside her and it throbbed in time with her heartbeat. Jesse's hands dropped from her waist to her hips, then swept beneath the short hem of her skirt to explore the curve of her behind with wide, callused palms. Jillian groaned in the back of her throat and held him more tightly.

He caressed her rear with long, sure strokes until she was quivering in his grasp. Jillian's breath staggered in her lungs. It was as if she were actually living one of the dreams she'd been having the last few weeks. Only better. *Much* better. He was so tall, so strong, so overwhelming to every one of her senses, she could hardly think straight.

When he tore his mouth from hers and looked down into her eyes, he blew out a breath. "I had to have that taste of you," he admitted, voice rough and low.

"I'm glad," she said, then stroked her fingertips along his jaw.

"Yeah. I hate to say it, but we've got to go to that damn party." He ran one hand through her hair, letting the silky strands slide through his fingers. "And if we don't go now..."

Jillian dropped her forehead to his chest and fought for air. Kissing him had opened up a whole new world of sensation for her and she was shaking in response. She wanted more. But she knew he was right.

"You're right," she said, lifting her gaze to his. "We should go. Besides, I think I need a drink."

He grinned briefly. "You are not alone."

The Texas Cattlemen's Club was crowded, noisy and decorated with black and white balloons and hundreds of strings of tiny white lights. Waiters moved through the mob of people like ballet dancers, balancing silver trays loaded with either canapés or flutes of champagne. Music streamed from the far end of the great room where a local five-piece band played on a stage.

Jesse supposed it was a good party, and he knew this one night would raise thousands of dollars for the Royal Health Clinic. Still, he thought, as he looked at the beautiful woman on his arm, he wished the evening were over so they could be alone again. That kiss still burned through him. His body felt tight and if he didn't keep his mind off the taste of Jillian, he wouldn't be able to walk.

"It looks beautiful," she said, looking up at him, eyes shining, wide, delicious mouth curved in a smile.

"No, it looks nice. You're beautiful." She just stared at him, her eyes warm and soft, and Jesse had to tear his gaze from hers before he gave in to that nagging urge to taste her again. "How about some champagne?"

"Sure. Thank you."

He stopped a passing waiter, took two glasses from him and handed one to Jillian.

"It looks like half the town is here," she said, leaning in to make sure he could hear her over the crush of conversations and swell of music.

"That sounds about right," he said, letting his gaze slide over the gathered crowd. He nodded to old friends, then spotted someone he thought Jillian should meet. "Come on. I'll introduce you to Will's wife."

"His wife? Oh, that's right. She was at the service, too. Who's the other woman?"

"Allison Cartwright."

"Megan, Allison, good to see you both," he said. "I wanted you to meet my new business partner, Jillian Norris."

Beside him, Jillian jolted, clearly surprised at his introduction.

He looked at her and whispered, "The whole town will know soon enough."

"You're right." She nodded and shook hands with both women.

"So what kind of business are you in?" Megan asked.

"I'm opening a pie shop."

"Oh, lovely," Allison said on a deep sigh. "I do love a good pie."

"That's a great accent," Jillian said, focusing on the lovely redhead. "Ireland?"

Allison grinned. "You've a good ear. Most don't guess right first off."

"Well, I'm from Vegas and we got visitors from all over the world, so I recognize different accents." She took a sip of champagne. "Have you moved here permanently, Allison?"

"I wish I could, but sadly, my visa is soon to expire."

"Oh, I'm sorry."

"So am I," Megan said and dropped one arm around Allison's shoulders. "We're going to try to get it extended, though, right?"

"Worth a try." Allison flipped her long red hair back over her shoulder. "I'm having a lovely time in your country. There's so much to see and do and I'm not nearly ready to go home yet."

"Hopefully you won't have to," Jesse said.

He took hold of Jillian's hand and she curled her fingers around his. That simple connection with her, the feel of her warm, soft hand was enough to awaken barely banked embers inside him.

Allison beamed at their joined hands and Jesse made a mental note to talk to Rand Gibson at some point about the woman's visa. Rand was second in command to Will as CEO at Spark Energy Solutions.

Will couldn't do it since he was still in hiding. So as much as Jesse hated getting involved in the business end of the family empire, it would be up to him to check on this.

But tonight wasn't about business. Tonight was to show Jillian around. He'd already noticed that every man in the room had watched her walking across the room. And he couldn't blame them. Hell, he could hardly take his eyes off her himself. That dress was designed to break a man. Her hair, long and wavy, was a golden blond temptation. Those heels she wore made her long legs look even longer than usual, and every time she took a breath, her breasts lifted beneath the deeply cut bodice and the view about stopped his heart.

And he couldn't get the taste of her out of his mind. The feel of her body pressed to his. The sigh of her breath against his cheek. Her eager response to his kiss. His body tightened, and Jesse silently wished they'd never left her tiny apartment.

He gave Jillian's hand a squeeze and held on. "I promised Jillian a dance, so if you ladies will excuse us…"

"Absolutely," Megan said, lifting her glass in a toast. "Enjoy yourselves."

The woman's smile was wistful, and Jesse understood why. He felt bad for Megan. She'd been sucked into the world's weirdest soap opera. But she was a standup, he'd give her that. She was sticking with Will and doing everything she could to help them find the bastard who had screwed with all of their lives.

But he wasn't going to think about any of that tonight, either. Jesse led Jillian through the crowd and idly noticed Rand Gibson standing in the shadows where he was close enough to have been listening in on the conversation he and Jillian had been having with Megan and Allison. Jesse frowned to himself. *Why the hell would Rand be eavesdropping?*

Shaking his head, Jesse took Jillian's champagne flute and together with his, left them on an empty table. Then keeping a firm grip on her hand, he threaded their way toward the dance floor. Several times he paused briefly along the way to introduce Jillian to different people. Everyone was excited by the idea of a pie shop opening on Main Street and that boded well for business. And, he told himself, once people tasted Jillian's pies, they'd be customers for life.

"Who's that?" Jillian poked his shoulder then discreetly pointed at a couple who were being toasted by a small crowd.

Jesse smiled briefly. "That's Knox McCoy and Selena Jacobs. They're just recently engaged, so that's a celebration."

"Aw, that's so nice." Jillian sighed a little, and he wondered what it was about talk of weddings that turned women into marshmallows.

On the dance floor, he swung her into his arms and began moving to the music, steering her smoothly into the steps.

"You're a good dancer," she said.

"Don't sound so surprised." Jesse slid his open palm up and down her bare back. "Cora Lee made sure both of her sons wouldn't stomp a girl's feet flat on the dance floor."

She laughed, tipping her head back to gaze up at him. "I knew I liked your mother."

He looked down into her eyes and fresh heat erupted between them. She took a breath and licked her lips, and Jesse nearly groaned. He was in a bad way here and fighting like hell to hold on to the few slippery threads of his control.

He trailed his fingers along her spine, and she shivered, her eyes going a little glassy. "I really like this dress," he said.

"Right now," she said softly, "I really like it, too."

"I don't think I even told you how beautiful you look tonight."

"You did. And just did again."

"It deserves repeating." He moved into a turn, holding her tightly, watching her long, silky hair fly out around her shoulders. "You puzzle me."

She grinned. "Isn't that a nice thing to say?"

"There it is again. Puzzlement."

"I'm an open book, Jesse."

He laughed. "Women always say that, but doesn't

matter if the book's open if it's written in a language you can't read."

"You seem to do all right."

He shook his head and looked into eyes that haunted him day and night. "No. There isn't a man alive who can translate that book."

She smiled, laid her head on his shoulder and followed his lead. The music flowed on from one song to the next without breaking stride, and so Jesse continued to glide across the floor, holding her pressed to him.

"Thank you for bringing me here tonight," she said quietly, lifting her head to look up at him. "I know you didn't want to come, but you did anyway."

"It was worth it to see you in that dress." His gaze locked on hers.

"You look very handsome in that tux."

One corner of his mouth lifted briefly. "The tux is a small price to pay for dancing with the most beautiful woman here."

"You're pretty smooth when you want to be, aren't you?"

"You bring it out in me."

"Not until tonight," she said, laughing.

"Well, a lot of things changed tonight."

She sighed a little and again chewed at that bottom lip. He'd noticed she did that a lot when she was nervous, or unsteady about something, and he was glad to know she was as on edge as he was.

"I guess so," she said, and shivered. "That kiss..."

Instantly, his body fisted. He trailed his fingers up and down her spine, enjoying the sparks in her eyes as she reacted to his touch. "Yeah, I'm thinking about that, too."

"What're you thinking exactly?"

"I'm thinking we should do it again as soon as we get clear of this place." He waited to see her reaction.

"And I think that's a great idea." She slid her hand along his shoulder to the back of his neck and ran her fingers through his hair.

He gritted his teeth, glanced around the crowded room, then shifted his gaze back to hers. "Then let's do some fast introducing you to a few more of these people and get the hell outta Dodge."

That smile of hers was all the encouragement he needed. Leading her off the floor, Jesse made stops at several groups of people. If his friends wondered about why he stopped to say hello and then left again seconds later, it didn't matter to Jesse. Jillian charmed them all and he watched with a weird sense of pride. She'd been dropped into a new town, without knowing a soul, and she was handling it all with a lot more confidence and style than most would have. She was stronger than she thought and that appealed to him on multiple levels.

She was creative and kind and ambitious. She was a damn good mother and a hell of a kisser. Everything he discovered about Jillian Norris made him want to learn more.

A part of him was bothered by that realization. As he'd told Will, Jesse wasn't in a position to offer Jillian all the things a man should. He already had a family he had to look out for because of his own carelessness. How could he promise someone else forever when he already owed a debt to his sister and her son that he could never repay?

A sinking sensation opened up in his gut as he watched Jillian smile and laugh at something Sheriff Nathan Battle said. His wife, Amanda, slapped her husband's forearm playfully, then leaned in and whispered something he didn't catch to Jillian.

Still smiling, Jillian looked up at him and everything in Jesse turned over. Her eyes, her smile, the fall of her hair and the touch of her hand all combined to twist Jesse up into so many different knots he couldn't begin to untangle them. All he knew for sure was that he wanted her more than his next breath.

Eight

Twenty minutes later, they were headed for the door. Jesse got her wrap and his hat, then led her out into the cool summer night. The black sky glittered with stars that not even the streetlights could dim. A soft wind shot down the street, lifting the ends of Jillian's hair and flipping at the hem of her skirt.

She laughed and admitted, "I won't remember half of the people I just met."

"You'll meet 'em again," he told her. "When they come to buy our pies."

"*Our* pies?"

He winked. "Partners, remember? For now."

For now.

Jillian told herself she'd do well to remember those two words if nothing else from tonight. And she wondered if he wasn't trying to tell her that more than their business partnership was "for now." What they felt when they were together wasn't a declaration of love buzzing between them. This was plain old-fashioned lust. Nothing wrong with that—as long as you didn't try to convince yourself it was something more.

A pang of regret jangled her nerves before she could stop it and she shivered a little as she tried to let it go.

"You're not cold, are you?"

"No, it's nice tonight."

He studied her in the dim glow of a streetlight, and Jillian tried to read what he was thinking, feeling, and failed. "If you've changed your mind about this, just say so. I'll walk funny for a week, but it's all right."

Shaking her head, Jillian reached up, cupped his face between her palms and drew him down for a kiss that seared them both. Lust or love, this was too big to ignore. She had to have him with her even if it was only for this one night.

His arms came around her like steel bands. He lifted her off her feet and a part of her thrilled to it. In the glow of a streetlight, he kissed her deeply, letting her know without words that he wanted her as badly as she did him. That was powerful and for tonight, it was enough.

When he finally tore his mouth free of hers and drew in a deep breath, he said, "It's been killing me, waiting to get another taste of you."

A laughing couple burst through the door behind them and Jesse reluctantly set her on her feet. "But this isn't the place for it."

Last chance, she thought. Last chance to change her mind and turn away from what she was feeling before it overwhelmed her. But even as she thought it, Jillian knew it was already too late to go back. Maybe it had been too late since the first day she'd met him.

"My apartment's close," she said, locking her gaze with his.

"Not close enough." He grabbed her hand and hurried to his black Range Rover.

The drive was a short one, but two miles had never seemed so long to her before. Sitting beside him in the warm darkness, every nerve inside her lit up. It had been a long time since she'd been with a man and she'd *never* been with one like Jesse. He was the quintessential cowboy. Strong, mostly silent and a kindness underlying his strength that made him darn near irresistible. And she was done trying to resist him.

He parked the car in her building's lot and in a few minutes, they were up the elevator, and through her front door. He closed it behind them, threw the lock, then picked her up and slammed her against the door. "Have to touch you. Now."

"Yes," she said on a breathy sigh.

"You in this dress? Driving me crazy all night. Especially," he said, "since I've already had my hands under your skirt and I know you're not wearing much beneath it."

She lifted her chin and turned her head to the side, giving him access to her throat. He dragged his mouth along the column of her neck, and Jillian held tightly to his shoulders. "They're black."

"What?"

"My panties," she said. "They're black."

He groaned and lifted her legs to hook them around his waist. Then he filled his hands with her bottom, squeezing, kneading until she whimpered as need whipped from a nagging ache to an overwhelming demand. Shifting his grip on her, he reached down to stroke the core of her and even through the silky fabric of her panties, Jillian shook with reaction. Spirals of pleasure and expectation coiled inside her, and she moved into his touch.

He dipped his head to the base of her throat, then lifted her higher against the door so he could taste the valley between her breasts.

"Jesse…" Breathless, she gasped for air and couldn't find any. Her heartbeat pounded in her ears and then he snapped the elastic band on her panties and she groaned.

He tossed the panties to the floor, then murmured, "Sorry about those."

"Don't care, don't care." Her head moved back and forth against the door. She hooked her legs tighter around him and arched into him, wanting, needing.

His thumb stroked that aching, throbbing core. She was wet for him and so hot she felt the fire inside spreading, threatening to incinerate them both. He pushed one finger, then two inside her, and Jillian cried out his name as she instantly splintered. Her body trembled with the waves of pleasure shaking through her and before they had ended, he withdrew his hand and worked at the button and zipper of his slacks.

Sighing, smiling, she looked into his eyes and said, "That was—"

"Just the beginning," Jesse promised and he pushed his hard length into hers with one sure stroke. Jillian moaned and took him in. He filled her so completely, so thoroughly, she couldn't have said where she ended and he began. And she didn't care. As long as he stayed inside her. Always. Higher, deeper, claimed her as no one else ever had.

She felt the cold of the door behind her back, but it meant nothing compared to the heat within. He was so big. So hard. His body locked into hers as if made to fit, and she wanted more. Her legs locked around his middle and her hips rocked furiously, keeping up with the rhythm he set.

"Take it all and let go," he whispered, fixing his gaze to hers.

She looked into his eyes, saw her own reflection there and was shocked by the naked desire etched into her face. Jillian had never known such wild desire. Such overpowering emotions and sensations crashing together inside her. Her body hummed, her blood rushed and as the tight tingle of expectation at her core expanded, she leaped into the fire.

Clutching his shoulders tightly, she called out his name and rode him hard as a climax bigger than anything she'd ever imagined roared through her. And still, he pounded himself into her, taking, giving, taking again until she couldn't think, couldn't speak, could hardly breathe and she didn't care.

His hands gripped her hips and she felt the impression of every one of his fingers against her skin. He held tight, looked into her eyes, then exploded into her body with a hoarse cry of release that shattered her every bit as much as her orgasm had.

They clung together like survivors of a shipwreck. Jillian was still pinned to the door behind her and Jesse was still deep inside her. Where she would keep him, if she could. Breath staggered in and out of her lungs and she held him as he buried his face in the curve of her neck and fought for his own breath.

"Couldn't wait another minute," he said tightly. "Took you against a damn door."

"And I loved every second of it," she assured him.

He lifted his head, looked into her eyes and said, "Yeah, me, too. But like I said, I wasn't thinking. And now it's time to pay. Didn't use a condom."

Her eyes went wide and her mouth dropped open. Jillian's fuzzy brain fought to focus on the situation, but it was so far out of her scope, it wasn't easy. She hadn't given a single thought to protection and that had *never* happened to her before. Even the night she'd gotten pregnant with Mac, she'd insisted the Will impostor use a condom. It was Fate's little joke that she'd gotten pregnant anyway. But tonight—
"Oh, God."

"That pretty much covers it." He pulled her into his arms, peeling her away from the door and disentangling their bodies.

Jillian didn't know which devastated her more—the knowledge that she'd been so completely reckless…or the loss of his body inside hers.

On her feet again, she pushed her hand through her hair and thought about where she was in her cycle, frantically figuring out if she was fertile or not. Finally, she said, "I think it'll be okay. I mean, I should be safe."

He scrubbed one hand across his face, then looked her directly in the eye. "If you're not, I expect you to tell me."

"Absolutely." She wouldn't keep something like that from him. "And you should know, I'm healthy."

"So'm I," he said quickly. "So one worry off the table."

Her knees were a little wobbly, so she walked across the room to her bed and sat down. The bed-springs squealed and she laughed. "I can't believe—" she shook her head and looked up at him.

"Yeah, that's something I've never done before. I wouldn't take chances, Jillian."

"I know that," she said, looking up at him.

"I can only say I lost control." Then he added wryly, "I'm not sorry."

"Me, either," she admitted as a fresh, pulsing need erupted inside her.

"Good." He reached for his wallet and pulled out two condoms. Showing them to her, he said, "Because I'm not done with you yet."

"Oh, I'm so glad to hear that."

He peeled out of his clothes while she slipped out of her dress and in seconds they were naked, rolling across the mattress to the accompanying shrieks from the bedsprings.

"Should've gotten you a better bed," he murmured as he lowered his head to her breast. He took her nipple into his mouth and lips, teeth and tongue working that hard, pink bud until she twisted beneath him.

"If it gets too noisy, we can move to the floor," she insisted, reaching down to close her hand around the hard length of him. She ran her fingertips up and down his shaft, scraping gently with her nails until he lifted his head and groaned.

"You keep touching me like that I'll go wherever the hell you want me to."

Jillian grinned. "Don't plan to stop."

She slid her foot up and down one of his legs. She loved the strength of him. The hard solid body, the husky whispers, the gentle touch. In fact, everything about Jesse reached something inside her she hadn't known existed. Jillian didn't want to think about what that meant. Didn't want to think at all right now. She wanted to lose herself in what was happening to her body. Revel in what he made her feel.

"You're thinking," he ground out, then ordered, "stop it."

She laughed, and he rolled onto his back, dragging her on top of him. Her hair fell down on either side of his face like a blond curtain, closing the two of them off from the rest of the world.

He looked up at her and said, "You take my breath away."

Jillian's heart leaped as she looked into his eyes and saw the fire for her burning brightly. She kissed him slowly, lingering over the taste of him and beneath her, she felt his heartbeat jolt into a gallop. Lifting her head, she met his gaze again and whispered, "You make me feel..."

Reaching down, he stroked her center and made

her gasp as fresh sensation rushed through her. "Jesse…"

"Can't get enough of you," he admitted. "Not sure I like admitting that."

She smiled in spite of the words because it was so Jesse. She reached over to the small bedside table, grabbed one of the condoms and tore the foil packet open.

Jesse's gaze flashed, and she smiled. Going up on her knees, she straddled him, then curled her fingers around the hard length of him. She smoothed the latex on with a slow, deliberate motion designed to torture them both.

"You're killing me," he said, hands on her thighs, gripping tightly.

"I'm just getting started," she said and lowered herself onto him. Her head fell back and her spine bowed as she took him deep inside. Reaching up, his hands covered her breasts, his fingers tweaking and pulling at her hardened nipples. Her moans mingled with his as she moved on him, setting a rhythm that pushed them both into a race for completion.

He dropped his hands to her hips and rocked beneath her, pushing even higher into her depths. Jillian groaned with every slick slide of his body into hers. His hands tightened on her hips and he used his own strength to help her move, to keep up the sharp, fast pace leaving them both breathless.

Jillian met his gaze and never looked away as she

began to move on him more quickly. She saw need burning in his eyes, felt it in the grip of his hands. That amazing chorus of sensations opened up inside her again and Jillian raced to meet it. To jump into that chasm filled with fire and light and explosions of pure pleasure.

Bedsprings shrieked and breathing sighed into the room as they moved as one, each of them striving to reach the conclusion they knew was coming. And when it did, Jillian shouted in surprise at the force of the climax slamming into her. She rocked wildly, drawing it out, making it last as long as possible and while her body was still trembling with release, Jesse leaped with her. The two of them tumbled into the abyss, holding tightly to each other to cushion their fall.

Jesse looked at the woman lying beside him on the loud, uncomfortable bed and knew he was in trouble. He'd thought that being with her would ease the need that had been clawing at him for weeks. Instead, all he could think about was having her again.

Before Jillian, the women in his life were like ghosts, appearing and disappearing from his world without leaving so much as a ripple in their wake. Jillian, though, had been causing nothing *but* ripples since the moment they met.

"Okay," she murmured, "now it's my turn to say I can hear you thinking."

His mouth twitched as he rolled to his side and propped himself up on one elbow to look down at her. God, she was beautiful. "All right, yes. I'm thinking."

She reached up and cupped his cheek in her palm. "You don't have to."

"Don't have to what?"

"Give me the speech." Her mouth curved and her beautiful eyes warmed.

There was a single light burning in the apartment and that soft, golden glow lay across her naked body like early-morning sunlight. "What speech is that?"

Smiling, she brushed her hair back from her forehead, then draped one arm across her belly. "You know the one. It starts off with *That was great, babe. But you know, I'm not the commitment kind of guy.*" She paused, then added, "And it always ends with *I'll call you.*"

Not much he could say to that since he'd given different versions of that speech too many times to count. This was the first time he didn't want to say any of it. And the one time it was most important to do exactly that.

"Jillian…"

"Relax, Jesse," she said, giving him another smile. "I don't need any promises from you. We both went into this knowing that it wasn't forever. I'm not going to beg you to stay."

Why the hell not?

And why did it irritate him that she was being so damn reasonable and understanding?

She laughed and shook her head. "You're insulted."

"What? No." He scowled. "Okay, maybe a little."

"We're business partners, right?" Jillian rolled out of bed, walked naked to the closet. He admired the view of that truly excellent butt and was disappointed when she reached into the closet, pulled out a short, pale blue robe and slipped into it.

She tied the belt at her waist, whipped her hair back over her shoulder and shrugged. "It's better for the business if we just forget all about tonight."

"Forget about it." He repeated it because he could hardly believe she was saying it. Jesse was pretty sure that tonight's festivities were burned into his brain. He'd have as much chance of forgetting what happened here as he would holding his breath for the next fifty years.

"Well, yeah." She walked to the bed, sat down on the edge and leaned in to kiss him. "This was great. I mean, really great. But I'm not expecting you to throw yourself at my feet pledging eternal love."

"Is that right?"

"Yes, it is." She tipped her head to one side and looked at him quizzically. "Do most women spend the night with you then start building wedding dreams?"

"No, but they're not usually in such a hurry to

brush me off, either." And he didn't much care for the feeling of being discarded. He had a momentary regret for the women he'd dismissed so easily and a touch more respect for the *one* woman who had taught him what the others had felt.

Jillian gave him an understanding smile and one more soft, brief kiss. "It's better this way, Jesse. No promises made, so none broken. We'll be partners—for now," she reminded him and he didn't much care for having his own words tossed back at him.

"And then?"

She stood up. "Then, we'll be friends."

He gritted his teeth and said, "I don't normally want to bend my friends over a table and—"

She inhaled sharply and interrupted him. "That's not helping."

"Not trying to help."

"Why not?" she asked. "Isn't this just what you wanted? If I hadn't said it first, wouldn't you have given me the speech?"

"A man can't have this conversation naked," he muttered and swung out of the bed to snatch up his pants. Tugging them on, he zipped and buttoned them before talking to her again. "Once I give that speech, I'm not 'friends' with the woman I've given it to."

"First time for everything," she said.

"I don't want to be your *friend*, Jillian."

She threw her arms up and shook her head. "Then what do you want?"

He looked into those grayish-green eyes and realized that what he wanted was her. Sex hadn't eased that desire, it had only inflamed it. So no, he wouldn't be her friend. He wouldn't be her lover, either. Or any other damn thing. Once their partnership was over, they'd have nothing between them.

And he didn't like how empty that made him feel.

"You. Damn it, I want *you*."

"Then don't go yet," she said, untying her robe.

He didn't.

Nine

Jesse dressed to leave a couple of hours later and he thought he'd never done anything more difficult than walking away from this woman when she lay there naked and warm, a soft smile on her face. And *that* was the main reason he had to go.

He'd told himself that sex with Jillian would clear his head, get her out of his system. Sadly, the reality was that she was deeper inside him now than she had been before.

"I've got to get back to the ranch," he said. "Gotta be up at dawn to get a couple of the horses ready to be sent home."

She nodded, held the sheet to her breasts and sat

up. Pushing that mass of blond hair back from her face, she murmured, "You don't owe me an explanation, Jesse. You don't owe me anything."

He scrubbed one hand across his face. "I don't want to hurt you."

"I know that. You won't."

Yes, he would, Jesse told himself. Because sooner or later, Jillian would start expecting more from him. She would start looking at what was between them as a relationship. Strong and smart, she was still female, and every woman he'd ever known eventually started looking for promises. And he couldn't do that.

Because when he made a promise, he kept it. So he was careful with what he said. He couldn't give Jillian and little Mac what he already owed to his sister's son and the memory of the father that little boy had lost.

With that thought firmly at the front of his mind, he picked up his hat and jammed it onto his head. "Guess I'll see you."

"Yes, you will. Tomorrow," she said. Then she laughed. "Don't look so panicked, Jesse. I'm not going to the ranch to hunt you down. Just to pick up Mac."

Idiot. "Right. I'll see you then." He walked to the door, opened it and looked back at her. "Lock this after me."

She was smiling as he left and Jesse told himself

to make sure he was nowhere near the ranch when she arrived to pick up her little girl.

Two days later, Lucy and Jillian were outside the empty shop that would soon be filled with the scent of baking pies. She should be looking at the shop with Jesse, Jillian thought. He was her partner, after all. But she hadn't spoken to him since the night they'd been together.

If he was avoiding her, then he was doing an excellent job of it.

"I'm so glad Jesse helped you get this started," Lucy said as Jillian opened the door with the key provided by the real estate agent. "A little surprised, but glad."

"Surprised why?" Jillian asked, looking over her shoulder at her friend.

Shrugging, Lucy continued. "He's more of a stand-back-and-observe kind of guy. This is the first time I remember him doing anything like this."

Jillian thought about that for a moment and told herself it didn't signify anything. He was being kind, that was all. When she paid back his investment, the shop would be all hers and that would probably be the end of her time with Jesse.

Of course, since she hadn't heard from him in two days, maybe her time with him had already ended. There was no way to know and that was making her a little nuts even though she knew it shouldn't.

Jillian thought about that night with Jesse and everything she'd said to him. And how much it had cost to squeeze the words out past the knot in her throat. She'd told him it would be better if they both simply forgot that night, while her mind had been screaming at her that she would never forget. What she'd found in his arms was something she'd never thought to have. Knowing it wasn't hers to keep had torn at her even as she pretended to be untouched by it all.

She didn't want to love him, so she wouldn't allow herself to even consider the word. Hadn't she learned the hard way that men didn't stay? That love was something you found in a book but only rarely in life? Jillian had Mac to think about now and that was where she would put her focus—and not on the man who touched her heart, her soul, her mind.

Chewing at her bottom lip, Jillian reminded herself that *she* hadn't contacted Jesse in the last two days, either. Maybe she should have rather than wait for him. Was it cowardly to stand back and say nothing? But pride had to come into this at some point, right? Why should she be the one to go see him? To call him? He could have come to her. Talked to her. But he hadn't. And that meant what?

"So what do you think?"

"I think he could have called," Jillian grumbled. "Or said *something*."

Lucy's eyebrows shot up. "Well, blurted truths are

always so interesting. But what I meant was, what do you think of the shop?"

Oh, God. Rolling her eyes, Jillian said, "Sure. I knew that." She looked around the interior of the shop and smiled. It was clean and had enough room for a few tables and chairs. There was a gleaming glass display case, an old-fashioned cash register and through the swinging door, she assumed, the kitchen. She walked around behind the counter, just to get a feel for the place.

Standing there, she could look out at Main Street and watch people hurrying down the sidewalks. In a few weeks, those people would be coming in here. To her shop. She took a breath and tried to focus on the moment.

"I think it's perfect," she said, more to herself really than Lucy. "Of course, I'll want to paint, make it sort of cheery, and I need to get some tables and chairs for the front here. Maybe tiny bistro size?"

"Okay, let's have it."

She looked at Lucy. "Have what?"

"Please." Lucy snickered. "The kids aren't here. Jesse's not here. So talk."

She didn't want to talk. If she started, she might not stop and the truth was, what *could* she say? That Jesse and she had had a few hours together that had completely shaken her to her bones and now it was over? How sad was that?

"Nothing to say, Lucy. Honestly."

Her friend just watched her. Seconds ticked past. Lucy continued to stare, never saying a word. And Jillian couldn't take it.

"Fine. Stop the torture." She sighed and admitted, "I just haven't seen Jesse in a couple of days and I thought he could have called or something and that sounds so junior high I'm embarrassed."

"He's in Houston."

"What?" Jillian stared at Lucy.

"Jesse had to drive a horse back to its owner. Most of our guys were out checking the herd and Carlos can't go because his wife is about to go into labor." Lucy shrugged. "So Jesse's been gone. I thought you knew."

"No," she mused, running her hand over the sparklingly clean white-and-gray marble counter. "He didn't tell me." But then why would he?

The more she thought about it, the more Jillian realized that Jesse was talking to her in his way. By *not* contacting her, he was sending a message. There was no real connection between them. What they had was attraction and some really great sex, but beyond that, they owed each other nothing.

"That's fine. That's good, really. Better." Jillian heard herself babbling and couldn't stop. "I mean, we're not a couple or anything. He doesn't have to check in with me and I don't have to call him or anything to report on the shop. Business partners. That's us. That's it. And I'm fine with this."

When she finally ran out of steam, the silence in the shop was overpowering. Shooting a look at Lucy, she asked, "You don't believe me, do you?"

"Nope."

"I'm not making any sense here, am I?"

"Nope."

"So I'm an idiot."

"Yep."

Jillian laughed and shook her head. "You're right. I am acting like an idiot. I keep swinging back and forth on what I'm thinking, feeling. I mean, I knew going in that Jesse and I didn't have a future, you know? That nothing serious was going to happen between us and yet..."

"You still hoped for it."

She looked at Lucy and sighed. "I guess so and that's ridiculous because I don't—"

Lucy snorted and held up one hand. "Don't even bother telling me you don't want or need love in your life." She shook her head and said, "It's the same sad song we all tell ourselves when we've been hurt too many times to want to take the risk again. But the real truth, is *everybody* wants love."

"You're a philosopher now?"

"I am a woman of many talents," Lucy said, smiling. "Like I can see that you had sex with my brother and that it was good."

Jillian sighed again.

"All details are happily accepted," Lucy said,

then kept talking as she walked across the room and pushed through the door into the kitchen. "No, wait. On second thought, no details. This is my brother we're talking about and I don't want to throw up in your shiny new shop."

Jillian was right behind her. "Agreed. No details."

"Fine. But the point is the Amazing Lucy also sees that you're in love with my brother."

"No." Jillian instantly denied that charge. She didn't look at her friend because it was easier to talk about this without meeting her eyes. Instead, she looked around the small but efficient kitchen and smiled. "I mean, of course I care for him. Who wouldn't? Jesse's kind and gruff and funny and strong. He's wonderful with Mac and so patient, too, and—"

"Wow. Yeah I can hear how much you *don't* love him." Lucy opened one of the ovens, ran a finger over the door and inspected it. "Clean."

Oh, God, was Lucy right? Was it too late for her already? Jillian took a breath and asked, "Why are you so determined to have me love Jesse?"

"Because he deserves it," Lucy said, shutting the oven door. Turning around to face Jillian, she continued. "He deserves *you*. And Mac. I've never seen him as captivated by anyone as he is by you. He loves that little girl. He found this shop for you to help you with your dream. He's a good guy, Jill."

"I know that."

"And you deserve him." Lucy planted both hands on her hips. "For pity's sake, your eyes light up when you see him, you practically drool when he walks into the room…"

"I don't drool." Did she?

"That's metaphorical drool, but still…"

Even if she did feel more for Jesse than she was willing to admit, the bottom line was, "I can't risk it, Lucy. I've got Mac to think about."

Surprised, Lucy demanded, "You think he'd hurt that little girl?"

"Of course not." Jillian walked through the kitchen, too wound up to stand still. Too worried about what she was feeling to really take those emotions out and look hard at them. "He'd never do anything to deliberately hurt her. But—"

"I get it," Lucy said. "I've got Brody and I know what it is to worry about someone more than yourself. But what if you're just cheating Mac out of having a great father?"

As Lucy's question echoed in her mind, Jillian sighed, checked the cupboards, the cooling racks and the small bathroom at the back of the shop. It was perfect. And Jesse had arranged it for her. He'd had professionals in to clean the place top to bottom so she wouldn't have to worry about it. He'd become her *partner* so that she wouldn't have to wait years to make her dreams come true.

He'd said once that when he made a promise, he kept it. Did that mean she could trust him?

"You're overthinking this."

She looked at Lucy and said wryly, "I can't seem to stop."

"Well," her friend said, dropping one arm around Jillian's shoulders, "let me help. Jesse's in Houston so you can't do anything about any of this until he gets back. Right?"

"Yes..."

"So let's keep busy. We'll buy some paint and start working on the shop."

"I don't know." Truthfully, she had so much spinning through her mind, Jillian didn't know if she could be trusted with a paintbrush.

"Trust me." Lucy gave her shoulders a squeeze. "The kids are at the day care. We can probably get the whole front of the shop done in a couple of hours."

"I guess we could do that."

"Excellent." Lucy grinned. "You know I love shopping!"

Laughing, Jillian followed her friend out of the shop, locking it behind her. If it made her a coward to be grateful she could put off facing Jesse for another day, she was willing to accept the label.

The following day, Jesse was back from Houston and felt like he'd been dragged behind the truck the whole way. He hadn't had a decent hour's sleep since the night he'd left Jillian. No matter what he did, she was there, in his mind, refusing to be ignored.

He'd believed he could step back from her. But clearly it was going to take longer than he'd thought it would. What he needed to do was keep busy. Lose himself in the ranch, the work.

"Yeah, because that's working so well," he muttered as he walked across the ranch yard toward the main house. It took everything he had to not grab his damn cell phone and call Jillian. He could tell himself that he just wanted to check in, make sure everything was all right. But the truth was, he just wanted to hear her voice.

He was still muttering when he opened the front door and stepped inside. Instantly, his sister called out, "Jesse? Is that you?"

"Yeah."

"Well, thank God." She sounded irritated and impatient, but that wasn't anything new for Lucy.

"Jesse..." Mac's voice came as a plaintive wail that had him hurrying toward the great room.

"What's going on?"

"Hi, Uncle Jesse!"

"Hi, kid," he said, smiling at his nephew, playing with his trucks on the floor near his mother.

Lucy was sitting on the couch, a clearly unhappy Mac on her lap. His sister looked harried, Mac looked miserable and Jesse figured he looked confused.

"What's going on?"

"Mac's sick," Brody offered, never looking up from his trains.

"Sick?" he echoed.

"Sick," Mac whined.

"Come and take her," Lucy ordered, even as Mac held up both arms and wailed his name again.

"What's wrong with her? Where's Jillian?" He scooped the little girl into his arms while he looked around the room as if half expecting the woman to pop into existence. He was disappointed when that didn't happen.

"Jill had to work today," Lucy said, sweeping both hands through her hair. "Since she's quitting so soon after being hired, she felt bad about staying home with Mac and they were short-handed at the day care today, so she had to go in even though Mac's sick…"

"What kind of sick?" he asked, taking a quick look at the tiny girl in his arms.

"Sick, Jesse," Mac whined, laying her head on his shoulder.

Now that he was taking a good, hard look at her, he could see that her eyes were too bright and her cheeks were flushed. And a jolt of fear shot through him. "What's wrong with her? Did you take her to the doctor? Should I?"

Lucy grinned. "Calm down, oh, rational one. She's fine. She's just got a little fever and she's feeling pretty crappy."

"Crappy," Mac echoed.

"Oops," Lucy said with a grimace. "Anyway, I told Mac I'd keep her here, but she's been so restless, and all she wants is *you*."

Both pleasure and panic shot through Jesse in a split second. Pleased that the child had asked for him, even though he had no clue what to do for a sick kid. He patted Mac's back gently and felt his heart clench when she gave a tired sigh and snuggled in closer to him.

"You're panicking and it's not very attractive," Lucy told him.

Jesse ignored that. "What am I supposed to do for her?"

"Just hold her and keep her comfortable."

"Right." How hard could that be? God, he really wished he'd had a little sleep in the last couple of days. "Okay, I'm taking her over to my place. I've got to get a shower and—" he broke off. How could he do that when he had to take care of Mac?

Lucy read his mind again. "Go on. I'll ask one of the guys to carry the crib to your house. Just lay her down when you take a shower. Maybe she'll sleep for you. She should be tired."

"Tired," Mac whimpered, and rubbed her eyes with a tiny hand.

"Okay sweetie," he whispered, "we'll go lay down."

Lucy smiled at him. "Don't look now, but you're sounding like a Daddy."

He fired a look at her. “Don’t get any ideas, Lucy. I mean it.”

“Oooh, your stern expression.” She held up both hands. “Color me terrified. Go. Go home. One of the guys will be there in a few minutes with the crib.”

Jesse left the house with a sick child on his shoulder and a block of ice in the pit of his stomach. He was being drawn deeper and deeper into the lives of Jillian and Mac. Now he had a baby girl looking to him for comfort. How could he walk away from that?

And what was it going to do to him when he finally had to?

By the time Jillian arrived at the ranch, she was tired, on edge and worried about Mac. Lucy had called her at work to say that Jesse was home and taking care of the baby. It had made her feel better to know that Jesse was with Mac because she knew how much her daughter loved the man. But at the same time, it was awkward because of the way things had been left between she and Jesse.

Now, she wasn’t sure what to expect when she walked into Jesse’s house. Late afternoon sunlight poured through the door with her entry and lay across the wood floor like a path Fate wanted her to follow.

“Jesse?”

“In here,” he answered, his voice quiet, soft.

She walked into the great room and dropped her

purse onto the first chair she passed. The room was dim, but there was enough light for Jillian to see Jesse lying down on one of the couches, Mac asleep on his chest. He looked at her and held one finger to his lips for silence.

His hair lay across his forehead, he had one arm around her baby girl, keeping her steady. He smiled at Jillian and her heart turned over. Just like that, it was done. The final tumble.

She was in love.

Maybe she had been all along. Who could resist a man who not only turned your blood into lava but was strong enough to be gentle and sweet with a child? This wasn't good and she knew it. Jillian hadn't been looking for love and she knew Jesse wasn't interested in anything remotely resembling a relationship, so there was nothing ahead of her but pain.

Yet, she couldn't regret this feeling. There would be plenty of time for regrets in the future. For this moment alone, she was going to enjoy the sensation of having her heart stolen. All the years she'd spent protecting her heart now felt like she'd really only been waiting. For Jesse.

"She just fell asleep," he said, stroking Mac's back.

"I should get her home." And get herself away from Jesse before she revealed too much.

"There's a crib here. Let her sleep."

Jillian kept her gaze locked with his and she saw that he wanted her to stay. She wanted it, too, but how could she hide what she was feeling from him?

While she stood there, frozen with indecision, he stood up, moving carefully, holding Mac close. Looking at him, Jillian felt the last of her resolve drain away. She didn't want to leave. She'd missed him for days. She loved him. She wanted to be here. With him. For as long as she could.

"Will you stay?" he asked.

Looking into his chocolate-brown eyes, she knew there was only one possible answer. "Yes."

With Mac asleep in her crib, Jesse and Jillian went into his bedroom just across the hall.

"Can we hear her?" Jillian whispered as he unbuttoned her shirt. His fingers brushed her skin and she sucked in a gulp of air.

"Both doors are open," he whispered back, "we'll hear her."

Jesse's bedroom was a male bastion. Browns, beige and forest green were the colors, and Jillian thought it was almost like bringing the outside in. The bed was wide and covered in a dark brown duvet. There were two chairs pulled up in front of a small, green-tiled fireplace, bookcases on either side of the room and photos of the ranch framed and hanging on the walls. The bedside lamps were brass and there were French doors that led onto the stone porch.

And there was Jesse. Jillian stared up into his eyes and wondered how she could ever have tried to convince herself that she wasn't in love. She threaded her fingers through his hair as he backed her toward the bed. He laid her down on the mattress then stretched out beside her.

She laughed a little. "How did we get naked so fast?"

"It's a gift," he said and bent his head to kiss her.

Their first time together had been a feverish, desperate joining as they each reacted to the tension that had built between them for weeks. Tonight, there was no fever, just the swamping need. She saw desire in his eyes and wished she could see more.

"You're thinking," he chided when he lifted his head to look at her.

"Make me stop," she said and took his face between her palms. He kissed her again, and Jillian's mind blanked out. How could she possibly gather thoughts or worries when his mouth was on hers? When his hands were sliding up and down her body?

He touched her everywhere, as if burning every line of her body into his mind. She ran her hands over his chest, marveling at the muscled, bronze skin and the warm feel of it beneath her palms.

She watched him, wanting to remember every moment of this night. If she didn't have a tomorrow with him at least she would have this memory. Expectation coiled deep inside her as they moved together, skin to skin, hands stroking, mouths tasting. Her breath came fast and short when he moved over her and when he pushed himself home, Jillian gasped, arching her back, moving with him in a silent dance of desire.

Outside, the sun died and the darkness crept into the room, enfolding them in a deep, shadow-filled quiet. They moved as one, each of them pushing the other toward the edge and as she climbed, Jillian held on to him, arms around his neck, legs around his hips. When her body splintered into thousands of jagged shards, she had Jesse to anchor her. She held him as she trembled, then held him tighter as he joined her.

A few minutes later, Jesse lay on his back and held her to his side. "I missed you."

He didn't sound happy about admitting it, either. Still, she tipped her head back to look at him. "I wondered where you were."

"I meant to call…"

"No," she said, watching his eyes, "you didn't."

Now he stared down at her, frowning. "I didn't?"

"No." She trailed her fingers across his chest, feeling the solid thump of his heart. "You didn't want to miss me, Jesse. Didn't want to call me. You were trying to let me know that what we had that night was all there was going to be."

His frown deepened. "And how did I feel about you staying here tonight?"

He was irritated, and she couldn't have said why she found that a little entertaining, even under these circumstances. "You wanted me in your bed, but you don't want me getting comfortable."

"Well, I sound like a real dick, don't I?"

Surprising herself, Jillian laughed a little. "No, you don't. You just don't want to love me."

He eased up onto his elbow and looked down at her. Jillian touched his cheek, then let her hand fall back. "I know how you feel. I didn't want to love you, either. But I do."

He froze. It was the only word she could think of to describe what happened to him the minute the *L* word was mentioned. It was as if he wasn't even breathing. His eyes flashed and those golden flecks shone in the dimness like spotlights.

"No, you don't."

"You don't get to tell me what I'm feeling," Jillian said.

"Why the hell not?" he demanded. "You just told me what I was thinking and feeling."

"Yes," she said sadly, "but I was right and you're wrong. I *do* love you."

"Stop saying that."

"Silence won't change anything. Even if I never say it again, you'll always know I feel it." She'd known it would go this way and still Jillian had

had to tell him. Love, when it finally arrived, just shouldn't be ignored or dismissed.

"I don't want you to," he said, sitting up and dragging her up with him. "There's no future for us here, Jillian."

"I didn't ask for a future, Jesse," she reminded him. "I haven't asked you for anything. What I'm feeling—"

"Don't—"

"It's a gift." She shrugged and smiled in spite of everything. "I was afraid to love, too. Every man I've ever known has walked away from me."

"Jill..."

"I told you my grandmother raised me," she said and took one of his hands in hers. She rubbed her fingers across his palm, feeling the calluses and scars he'd earned through a lifetime of hard work. Jesse wasn't a quitter. Jesse gave his word and kept it. Jesse was the kind of man you could count on.

She wished he was hers. Looking up into his eyes she said, "My parents decided they didn't much like having a child, so they left."

"Jillian—"

"First my dad. I was really young and two years later, my mom left, too. Grandma Rhonda was my rock then."

"I'm sorry..."

"I don't need you to be sorry. I just want you to understand. I was engaged once, but he left, too. And then I met Rich, pretending to be Will, and I was so hungry to feel something, to love someone, I let him sweep me off my feet in spite of the fact I should have known better. Then he left, too."

He gritted his teeth and swallowed hard, but he didn't interrupt her again.

"So when I met you, I told myself that you would be just like every other man in the world." She smiled sadly. "But you weren't. You aren't. And Mac saw it in you before I did." Laughing a little, she said, "Mac loved you first. But I couldn't. I didn't trust myself. Or you. But Jesse..."

She reached out to cup his cheek and only flinched a little when he pulled his head back. Sighing, she let her hand drop to her lap. "Jesse, you're the one."

"I can't be, Jill—"

"I like you calling me that," she said. "And as for me loving you, it's too late. It just is. My love doesn't depend on you loving me back or even on us being together. It's just there."

He got up, walked to the fireplace and slapped one hand on the mantel to stare down at the cold, empty hearth. "I can't do this. Be what you want."

"You *are* what I want."

He shot a hard look at her over his shoulder. "I've got a debt to pay. To Lucy. To Brody. I can't claim a life for myself when their lives are broken because of *me*."

She scooted off the bed, walked to him and asked,

"Are you talking about the accident? Lucy told me about it."

"Did she tell you it was my fault? That Dane died because I wasn't careful enough?"

"No, of course not." Jillian reached out to lay one hand on his shoulder and she could feel the tension in his body. "She doesn't think that, Jesse."

"Whether she does or not, I know it's true and that's enough."

"Jesse, it's crazy to blame yourself for a horrible accident."

"Yeah? What if something happened to Mac? Would you be so willing to forgive and forget then? What if I let her get hurt?"

He was so embroiled in his own guilt, there was no reaching him. No way to convince him that what had happened to Dane hadn't been his fault. He was too determined to punish himself for it.

And still, she tried.

"I would know," she said, "that you would always do everything in your power to protect those you love. You're not God, Jesse. You don't get to make the big decisions. The world is not a safe place. People get hurt. They die."

"Not because of me," he muttered thickly. "Not again."

Jillian's heart ached and she felt as if she'd been wrapped in ice. She was cold, head to toe, and knew that she'd never really be warm again. Because loving Jesse wasn't enough. She wanted him to love her back. Wanted the whole dream.

And she wasn't going to get it.

"It's over between us, Jillian," he said and his voice was so tight, so deep, it seemed to reverberate in the air around her. "Best if we just don't see each other anymore."

She rocked on her heels, shocked at how quickly this night had gone from beautiful to awful. "What about our partnership?"

Nodding, he said, "That doesn't change. I'll help you get the shop and I wish you luck with it."

"Wow. Thanks."

His head whipped up and his gaze bored into hers. "What the hell do you want from me?"

"You already know the answer to that."

"And I told you why that's not going to happen."

"You gave me excuses, Jesse. Not a reason."

Even in the darkness, she saw his eyes glitter. "I gave you all I can."

"No, you didn't," she said, shaking her head. "But that's your decision and we'll both have to live with it, won't we?" She took a deep breath then added, "If it's okay with you, I'll spend the night in the guest room with Mac." She stepped back, putting some distance between them. He didn't notice because he hadn't looked at her again. "I'd rather not wake her up."

He nodded. "That's fine."

She gathered up her clothes and walked out of the room. But on the threshold she stopped for one more look at him. He was standing as he had been. Alone. In the dark.

"I was wrong, Jesse," she said softly. "I guess you are just like every man I've ever known. You're walking away, too."

Ten

The next couple of days passed in a blur of activity.

Jillian's heart was bruised and battered, but she buried her pain by focusing on Mac and on the shop she was about to open. If her thoughts wandered to Jesse a few dozen times a day, she pushed them aside as quickly as she could.

During the day, she could manage. It was her dreams at night that kept tripping her up. She dreamed of him holding her, smiling down at her, kissing her. She woke up with the taste of him in her mouth and had to choke down fresh pain every morning.

It didn't help that her baby girl kept asking for

Jesse. Mac couldn't understand why her favorite person was gone from her life and trying to explain to a nearly two-year-old was a lesson in futility.

Just that morning, Jillian had been getting Mac ready to go when the little girl put both hands on her mother's cheeks.

"See Jesse?"

Pain, sharp and fresh, stabbed at her heart as she said, "No, sweetie. We're going to the day care. You can play with your friends..."

"See Jesse. Horsies." Mac's little mouth turned mutinous.

"We can't, baby."

"Mama, Jesse."

"Jesse can't play today, baby, so we're just going to go to work, okay?" *Please be okay with this*, Jillian pleaded silently. She hoped Mac stopped looking for Jesse soon, because she hated the thought that her daughter was in as much pain as she herself was.

One tear rolled down Mac's cheek, and Jillian scooped her up for a tight hug meant to comfort them both.

Of course, it hadn't. How could it, when they were both missing the same man?

Sighing, Jillian went back to stacking the order of pie plates that had been delivered just that morning. For now, she was going with standard, aluminum pie plates. But one day, she wanted to invest in personalized pie tins with the name of the shop stamped on them. Then she could offer people a discount on their next pie if they brought in the used tins.

She could see just how the shop would be and Jillian really wished she was more excited about it. She'd thought about doing this for years and now that it was here, it was shadowed by the loss of Jesse.

"Stop it," she ordered grimly. "Stop wishing and thinking and start *doing*."

With that thought firmly in mind, Jillian continued stacking the plates and let her mind wander to everything else that still needed to be done. She had her tables and chairs—she'd found them at an outdoor living shop. Wrought-iron, the tables had glass tops and were just big enough for two or three people to share comfortably and the matching chairs were perfect. Getting them set up in the front of the shop had made everything feel immediate. Real. The walls were painted a cheerful pale yellow and there were baskets of flowers hanging from the ceiling in the corners of the room.

Her supplies were ordered along with the kitchen tools she'd need to make this dream a reality. Without Jesse's help, she wouldn't have been able to do this and she knew it. She only wished he were there to see it happen. But it seemed you could only have *part* of a dream.

Jillian made lists of her lists just to keep everything in order. She kept records of every penny spent on her laptop along with projections of what would need to come next. There was so much to buy, not to mention the employees she'd have to hire. But that was a worry for another day. Right now, she had to set up the kitchen just the way she wanted it.

Since Jillian was still working half days at the day care—at least until they found someone to replace her—she was able to leave Mac there while she worked at the shop.

"Thank God," she murmured, because trying to work while keeping Mac out of trouble would have been impossible.

As she finished with the last of the pie tins, Jillian gave herself a mental pat on the back. And a second later, she heard the front door open and Lucy's voice call out, "Hey, Jill, are you in here?"

A sinking sensation opened up in Jillian's chest. She hadn't spoken to Lucy since the breakup with Jesse. Avoiding her friend hadn't been easy, but she hadn't wanted to put Lucy in the middle. And now, she didn't have a clue what she would say to her. But there was no way to elude Lucy today. "In the kitchen."

Lucy bustled in, carrying a cardboard tray with two cups of coffee and a bag from the diner. She wore jeans, boots and a dark red top. Her choppy brown hair was wind ruffled and her eyes pinned Jillian. "Hi, stranger! Thought you could use a break. I brought doughnuts."

"God, that sounds great," Jillian admitted. She

hadn't had much of an appetite the last week, but a doughnut was always good.

"Good. Let's go try out the new chairs and table out front." Lucy turned around and headed out, talking as she went. "I love them, by the way. I'm devastated that I was not included in the shopping trip, but I can forgive—as long as you call me for the next excursion."

"I know I should have called you," Jillian admitted. "It's just—"

Lucy set the coffees down and spread some napkins on the table before laying out the doughnuts. "No problem. Well, of course there's a problem, but I know it's not me. It's undoubtedly my brother.

"Plus," Lucy added, breaking off a piece of rainbow sprinkle doughnut and popping it into her mouth, "said brother has spent the last two days with the lovely personality of a bear with a jagged thorn in its paw. He's infuriated so many people, all of the cowboys are avoiding him and Carlos is threatening a walkout if Jesse doesn't stay away from the stables."

Jillian smiled.

"Ah. This pleases you." Lucy nodded sagely. "Completely understandable because he's probably the one who caused whatever it is that happened. Since I haven't talked to you in forever, I brought doughnuts to bribe you into telling me what's going on. So spill."

Jillian slumped onto the chair opposite her friend.

She could pretend otherwise, but why bother? For two days now, her heart had ached and she'd been walking in a fog of misery, so why not share it with the one woman she knew would understand? "It's a mess, Lucy. All of it."

She reached across the table and patted Jillian's hand. "Have a doughnut. Sugar is a cure-all. And then tell me."

Taking a sip of coffee, Jillian had a bite of doughnut and felt the sugar rush. Maybe Lucy had a point. "It's my fault."

"I doubt it."

Smiling sadly, Jillian said, "Oh, it is. I told him I love him and that's when everything went to hell."

Lucy sighed and took a sip of coffee. "It's so disappointing to find out my brother is a moron." Waving one hand in a "come on" motion, she prodded, "Tell me."

So Jillian did. She told her friend the whole story and in talking about it, she felt as if a blister on her soul had popped and she could take a breath easier than she had all week. Finally, she said, "He told me he can't be with me and Mac because he owes too much to you and Brody."

"What?" Clearly stunned, Lucy asked, "What the hell does that mean?"

"He blames himself for your husband's death."

"Of course he does," Lucy muttered, shaking her head. "You know, when our father died, Jesse was sixteen. As the oldest, he immediately appointed himself the 'man of the house' and started in on trying to manage all of us. Mom finally put a stop to that, but she couldn't make him see that the family and the ranch weren't solely his responsibility." She crumbled a piece of doughnut until it was crumbs and sprinkles, then stared at the mess.

Eventually, she lifted her gaze to Jillian's. "When Dane died, I was the one racked with guilt. If I hadn't gone along with his idea to be a part of the ranch, he'd still be alive. If I'd moved with him to Houston, he wouldn't have died. I drove myself crazy for a while until Mom stepped in and made me see that it was just an accident. If we'd lived somewhere else, maybe it would have been a car wreck that took Dane. We'll never know."

"Jesse believes he could have stopped it."

"That's because Jesse still believes he's the Grand Poo-bah of the Universe." Scowling, Lucy added, "I've told him and told him that Dane's death wasn't his fault, but he won't accept it. And still, I never thought he'd take this so far."

Now Jillian had guilt gnawing at her. "Lucy, I didn't mean to make you feel badly about this. It's not your fault."

"Oh," her friend said quickly, "no worries. I know *exactly* whose fault this mess is. Jesse is throwing himself on a pyre that only he can see. Idiot."

Jillian laughed a little and felt better than she had

in days. She should have called Lucy sooner. Should have trusted her friend to help her through this.

"You really do love him, don't you?" Lucy's question sounded wistful.

"I do. It would be so much easier if I didn't."

"Who wants *easy*?" Lucy shook her head. "Mom used to tell me that nothing great comes easy. So I'll take hard if I can have great at the end of it."

Jillian thought about it for a second. "I guess I would, too."

"Good," Lucy said with a chuckle. "Because I guarantee that life with Jesse will be hard. The man has a head like concrete."

"Lucy… Jesse was very clear. He's not interested." And Jillian wasn't going to wait and hope that things would change only to have her heart broken again. How many times could she recover from that kind of pain?

"Of course he's interested. Otherwise he wouldn't be such a bear right now. So don't give up," Lucy said, picking up her doughnut for a bite. "He's not the easiest man on the planet, but I think you love him enough not to care about that."

"It doesn't matter."

"Oh, Jill, love is the only thing that *does* matter."

Jesse swung the hammer so hard that when it made contact with the post, the entire fence shuddered. Taking a breath, he released it slowly, trying to control the frustration that had been simmering inside him for more than a week. But it was no use.

Since that last night with Jillian, Jesse hadn't been able to get a moment's peace. He kept seeing her face. Hearing her say he was like every other man in her life—letting her down. Walking away.

"Well, hell, can't she see I didn't *want* her to go?" He pulled another nail from the box lying on the ground, straightened up and swung the hammer at it. Solid, hard work should be giving him a sense of satisfaction. At least fixing loose boards on the corral fence allowed him to take out his aggravation on innocent nails.

But it wasn't helping.

He yanked off his cowboy hat and wiped his forehead with his forearm. Summer was settling in and it promised to be a hot one. He jammed the hat back onto his head and braced his forearms on the top rail of the fence. He stared off at the ranch yard and then let his gaze slide to his house. For the first time since moving into that place, Jesse hadn't been able to find any peace in it.

Because Jillian was there. Her image. Her scent still clung to the pillow beside his. Mac was there, too, as he could remember holding the little girl while she cried and slept. The crib was still in the guest room and he felt a pang every time he walked past it down the hall.

Now he wondered what was happening with them.

Was Jillian getting the shop put together? Was Mac still sick? And was he going to be doing this for the rest of his damn life? Wondering about the two people he loved because he wasn't with them to keep them safe?

Scowling, he went back to work. Lucy had left more than two hours ago and he knew his sister had gone into town to see Jillian. And he wished to hell he knew what they were talking about. "A hell of a thing, being jealous of your sister," he muttered and slammed the hammer home again.

He heard the car careening up the drive before he saw it. Lucy's truck was barreling toward the ranch house as if racing from a fire. Instantly, panic flared into life in the center of Jesse's chest. Was Jillian all right? Mac? Had something happened?

Jesse dropped everything and sprinted for the front of the house. Lucy jumped out of the truck, raced toward him and didn't have a chance to speak before he demanded, "Is Jillian okay? Mac?"

And just like that, Lucy's whole demeanor changed. Tension left her shoulders and a smirk twisted her mouth. "Well, that answers my question."

"What the hell are you talking about?" he demanded. "What question? Weren't you with Jill? Is she okay?"

"Jill's fine. So's Mac," she added, "not that you'd know since you haven't bothered to call her. Or to go see her."

"Damn it, Lucy," he ground out as his heart slowed from a gallop to a trot. "You had me thinking—"

"That they needed you and you weren't there?" Lucy finished for him. "Well, get used to that feeling because unless you wise up, you're going to be living with that."

"Why'd you drive in here like a bat out of hell? Just trying to scare ten years off my life?"

She leaned back against the side of her royal blue truck, crossed her arms over her chest and glared at him. "I was pretty sure you were in love with Jillian, but I wanted to be sure. Seeing your panicked reaction convinced me."

"Well, good for you." He turned to go because at the rate his temper was building, he didn't trust himself not to use the kind of language his mother would still give him grief over.

Lucy grabbed his arm and held him in place. "Why are you ignoring your family, Jesse?"

"What the hell does that mean?" He waved one arm as if encompassing the ranch and said, "I've been right here, all week, spending time with my family."

"I'm not talking about *our* family," she said, irritation spiking the tone of her voice. "I'm talking about the family you built with Jillian."

"Butt out, little sister." The warning came out as a growl. Lucy wasn't impressed.

"Not a chance. You *love* Jill, and you love Mac." Lucy shook her head. "They love you, too, so what the hell are you doing?"

"I can't do this. Can't talk about this with you."

"Why not?" Lucy lifted her chin and fixed her gaze on his, and Jesse had to silently admit that his younger sister had become a fierce woman. "You're using me and Brody as an excuse to deny yourself a life, so I think you can discuss it with me."

"I'm not—"

"Dane died." Two words that shook both of them.

Jesse heard the slight tremor in her voice before she covered it over in fury when she continued. "It wasn't your fault. It wasn't his fault. Or the damn horse's, either. It just happened. That's why they call things like that 'accidents.' You can't plan for it. You can't guard against it. It's just life, Jesse."

"I shouldn't have let him so close."

Lucy snorted a laugh. "Do you really believe Dane would have allowed you to keep him back? He was a city guy, but he was no coward."

"I didn't say he was."

"He was a good, kind, strong man who went after what he wanted." Lucy swallowed hard. "He died going after it, but it was important to him and he wouldn't have let you stop him."

Jesse thought back to his brother-in-law and conceded that she had a point. Dane had been just as hardheaded as the rest of them and determined to build a life on the ranch. He'd fought against Jesse's and Will's attempts to protect him and had goaded them and challenged himself in his quest to grab what he wanted most.

"Should I blame Dane, Jesse?" She looked up at him, shaking her head. "I could. I could say it was his fault for always pushing, doing too much. He shouldn't have rushed into things like he did, but he was so damn alive..."

"I'm sorry about Dane, Lucy. So damn sorry." Jesse shook his head, reached out and pulled his sister in for a hug. She wrapped her arms around him and squeezed.

"I know you are. So am I. But life keeps going, Jesse." She leaned her head back and looked up at him. "And if you don't wake up in time, life is going to pass you by."

He took a breath, easing the constriction in his chest. "But there's Brody to care for and—"

"Are you planning on moving off the ranch?" she asked.

"No."

"Then you'll be here for Brody. Just like you always are. And you can be here for Mac. And Jillian. And damn it, Jesse. Be there for yourself, too." She was frowning up at him and Jesse bent down to plant a kiss on her forehead.

"Since when did you get so damn bossy?"

"Since always and you know it."

"Yeah," he agreed. "But you didn't use to be right."

"Hah! I'm always right," Lucy teased. "You're just not willing to admit it very often."

He gave her another tight hug then let her go. Guilt would probably always be with him, Jesse silently acknowledged. But maybe for the first time since Dane's death, Jesse was coming to grips with it. Everything Lucy had said resonated with him and maybe if he'd really thought about it years ago, he'd have come to this conclusion sooner.

Dane had lived his life exactly as he'd wanted. Now, it was time for Jesse to go after what *he* wanted.

"I guess you're not the worst sister in the world…"

"High praise indeed." She hooked one arm around his waist as he turned toward the main house. "So, do you need some help picking out a ring?"

He pulled her hair. "Again, I say, butt out, little sister."

By late afternoon Jillian could admit that she was feeling a little better. She should have talked to Lucy sooner because that conversation with Jesse's sister had really done a lot to ease her pain. Maybe just being able to talk about the man she loved would be enough to help her transition into living without him.

Because no matter what Lucy said, Jillian couldn't afford to keep hope alive eternally.

"Jesse!"

Jillian sighed a little and looked at her daughter, sitting on the sidewalk beside her. Outside the pie shop, Jillian had been painting different designs on the display window, trying to figure out which one looked best. When she had it pinned down, she'd contact a professional sign painter to make it permanent.

"Not today, sweetie," she murmured automatically and looked up at the window. Miss Mac's Pie Shack. "There's your name, Mackenzie. You're on the window and maybe we could paint a little portrait of you, too. Use you as our logo, what do you think?"

"Jesse!"

Sighing, Jillian glanced at Mac again, noticed her daughter staring off down the sidewalk and lifted her gaze to see Jesse striding toward them.

Jillian's heartbeat clattered in her chest, making it almost impossible to breathe. He looked so good. Blue jeans, white button-down shirt, denim jacket and that black hat that never failed to set her pulse racing. "Oh, God…"

"Jesse!" Mac called it louder this time and took off down the sidewalk toward her hero.

"Mac!" Jillian started after her, but she needn't have bothered. Jesse swept the little girl up into his arms and then gave her the stuffed horse he'd brought for her.

"Mama, Jesse! Horsie!"

"I see that," she said softly, enjoying the flush of

pleasure on Mac's face and the bright light in her eyes as she stared at Jesse. Jillian's heart hurt. Jesse was only making this harder on Mac. The little girl had missed him so much that seeing him again would only freshen the pain when he disappeared again.

"Jill," he said, his gaze sweeping over her, up and down. "You look beautiful."

"No, I don't. I'm a mess." So of course he'd show up now. She wore jeans and a T-shirt and she had white paint on her cheek and her hair was pulled back in a ponytail threaded through the opening in a baseball cap.

"What're you doing here, Jesse?" Had Lucy talked to him? Had she made him see that sacrificing his own life as payment for something he thought was his fault was a waste? She wanted to hope but was too afraid to. She'd been hurt too many times.

He nodded, looked at the little girl in his arms, then back to Jillian. "Look, I understand that you might not be happy to see me right now, but I've got something I need to say to you. Then, if you want me to, I'll go and I'll stay away."

"Oh, Jesse, I think we've said it all."

"Not even close," he told her and took a step toward her. "When you told me you loved me, there was something I couldn't bring myself to say back to you. I want to do it now. I love you, Jillian. I love you so much it's a wonder to me."

She swayed in place as those three little words slammed home and took her breath away. “Jesse—”

“And I love Mac like she’s my own.”

“Jesse!” Mac hugged her horse, then laid her head on Jesse’s shoulder, patting his cheek with one tiny hand.

Jillian melted a little more. Her baby girl was happy. How could she not be?

“Without you, I can’t eat. Can’t sleep. My house is empty,” he said, “and my heart’s even emptier. Hell, Jill, until I met you, I was walking through life with my eyes closed. I swear, there was nothing but work and family.

“Then I met you and there was color and laughter and *life*, Jillian. There’s life where you are and I want that life.” He smoothed a strand of her hair back behind her ear. “I want it with you. And Mac. And however many more babies we can make together.”

“Babies?” she echoed.

“Babies!” Mac crowed and clapped her little hands.

Jesse grinned at the girl, then dipped one hand into his jeans pocket, coming up with a dark red velvet ring box.

Jillian gasped and felt tears fill her eyes until the box, Mac and Jesse were nothing more than blurs in front of her. Frantically, she blinked her eyes clear because she didn’t want to miss a moment of this.

“You’ll have to open it for me, since I don’t want to put our girl down…”

Our girl. Those two words rippled through her mind and heart, and Jillian felt love rise up to wash over her like a warm blanket on a winter night. Hesitantly, she opened the ring box, took one look and gasped again.

"Oh, Jesse..."

"I wanted you to have something different," he whispered. "Something as special as you are."

She stared at the ring unblinkingly. A star sapphire, surrounded by diamonds, it winked in the sunlight and seemed to shine with a hundred different colors deep in its center stone. Finally, she looked up at Jesse and saw at last what she'd longed to see in his eyes.

Love.

"I uh, stopped at the jewelry store on my way here. Didn't want to show up empty-handed. I love you, Jill," he said simply. "I love Mac. I want to adopt her officially, if you'll let me—"

"Jesse." She slapped one hand across her mouth.

"My dad wanted to adopt me and Lucy, but Mom didn't think it was fair to our biological father. So, if you want Mac to keep—"

"I think Mackenzie Navarro sounds perfect."

He smiled even wider. "Me, too." He kept talking then as if he were on a roll and reluctant to stop. "And I want you both to marry me and be with me forever. Help me build a life, Jillian. Let me help you build that future you've always dreamed of."

Slowly, she took the ring from its velvet bed, then slid it onto her finger. Jesse looked deeply into her eyes and whispered, "I will never walk away, Jillian. I will be with you. Always."

Tears stung her eyes again and her heart lifted so high in her chest it was a wonder her feet didn't leave the ground.

Then he took her hand and kissed the ring as if sealing a promise between them.

"I love you, Jesse," she said. "I think I always have. I know I always will." She looked at her little girl, lying so trustingly in his arms, a pleased smile on her tiny face. "Mac loves you, too, and you are exactly the father she deserves."

"So that's a yes," he said, more statement than question.

"Oh, absolutely it's a yes," Jillian told him, moving into the circle of his arms. "We will marry you, Jesse. And we will love you forever."

"Thank God," Jesse whispered.

"Thank God," Mac echoed.

"Oh, Mac," Jillian chided.

Laughing, Jesse held on to them, linking the three of them into a unit. He kissed Mac's forehead, and when Jillian tipped her face up to his, he kissed her lips, lingering just long enough to tell her that he'd missed her as much as she had him.

"I love you," he said, his gaze locked with hers, willing her to see. To believe.

And Jillian did. She reached up, cupped his cheek in her palm and whispered, "I love you, too."

While Royal bustled around them, the three of them stood together in front of the pie shop where dreams were born.

Staring into her eyes, Jesse vowed, "I've got my girls back and I swear to you, I will never let either of you go."

* * * * *

Don't miss a single installment of the
TEXAS CATTLEMAN'S CLUB:
THE IMPOSTOR.
Will the scandal of the century lead to love for these rich ranchers?

THE RANCHER'S BABY
by New York Times *bestselling author*
Maisey Yates.

RICH RANCHER'S REDEMPTION
by USA TODAY *bestselling author*
Maureen Child.

A CONVENIENT TEXAS WEDDING
by Sheri WhiteFeather.

EXPECTING A SCANDAL
by Joanne Rock.

REUNITED...WITH BABY
by USA TODAY *bestselling author*
Sara Orwig.

THE NANNY PROPOSAL
by Joss Wood.

SECRET TWINS FOR THE TEXAN
by Karen Booth.

LONE STAR SECRETS
by Cat Schield.

***

If you're on Twitter, tell us what you think of Harlequin Desire! #harlequindesire

SPECIAL EXCERPT FROM

HARLEQUIN® Desire

PR consultant Penelope Brand vowed to never, ever get involved with a client again. But then her latest client turns out to also be her irresistible one-night stand, and he introduces her as his fiancée.

Now she's playing couple, giving in to temptation...and might soon be expecting the billionaire's baby...

Read on for a sneak peek at
LONE STAR LOVERS
by Jessica Lemmon, the first book in the
***DALLAS BILLIONAIRES CLUB** trilogy!*

"You'll get to meet my brother tonight."

Penelope was embarrassed she didn't know a thing about another Ferguson sibling. She'd only been in Texas for a year, and between juggling her new business, moving into her apartment and handling crises for the Dallas elite, she hadn't climbed the Ferguson family tree any higher than Chase and Stefanie.

"Perfect timing," Chase said, his eyes going over her shoulder to welcome a new arrival.

"Hey, hey, big brother."

Now, that…that was a drawl.

The back of her neck prickled. She recognized the voice instantly. It sent warmth pooling in her belly and lower. It stood her nipples on end. The Texas accent over her shoulder was a tad thicker than Chase's, but not as lazy as it'd been

HDEXP0218

two weeks ago. Not like it was when she'd invited him home and he'd leaned close, his lips brushing the shell of her ear.

Lead the way, gorgeous.

Squaring her shoulders, Pen prayed Zach had the shortest memory ever, and turned to make his acquaintance.

Correction: reacquaintance.

She was floored by broad shoulders outlined by a sharp black tux, longish dark blond hair smoothed away from his handsome face and the greenest eyes she'd ever seen. Zach had been gorgeous the first time she'd laid eyes on him, but his current look suited the air of control and power swirling around him.

A primal, hidden part of her wanted to lean into his solid form and rest in his capable, strong arms again. As tempting as reaching out to him was, she wouldn't. She'd had her night with him. She was in the process of assembling a firm bedrock for her fragile, rebuilt business and she refused to let her world fall apart because of a sexy man with a dimple.

A dimple that was notably missing since he was gaping at her with shock. His poker face needed work.

"I'll be damned," Zach muttered. "I didn't expect to see you here."

"That makes two of us," Pen said, and then she polished off half her champagne in one long drink.